On the cover:
John Trumbull, Washington's aide-de-camp, painted this wartime image of Washington on a promontory above the Hudson River. Just behind Washington, his slave William "Billy" Lee has his eyes firmly fixed on his master. In the far background, British warships fire on an American fort.

Memoir of William Lee:
George Washington's Trusted Valet Earns His Freedom

By

George Coussoulos

A Legacy Book

Table of Contents

Author's Note

George Washington's views on slavery have been the speculation of his contemporaries, of historical scholars, and of generations of Americans who have both venerated his life and castigated perceived omissions. In truth, his views shifted over the course of his life – as might well be expected. The society of his childhood presented an environment where slavery was ubiquitous and natural. It was ingrained in the plantation structures of Virginia, and in 1732, the year of his birth; it was practiced in all thirteen of the English colonies. By the time he inherited Mount Vernon he was the legal owner of thirty-seven human beings in a state where over one-third of the population was enslaved.

In 1759 when Washington married Martha Dandridge Custis he increased the number of enslaved people at Mount Vernon to one hundred thirty-one. By the time of his death in 1799, three- hundred seventeen enslaved persons are counted in his ledger book. We know from extant records that he was neither shy about purchasing slaves nor selling them. Contemporary accounts describe the young master of Mount Vernon as treating his slaves "with more severity than any other man," and there is little dispute that he utilized harsh punishment against the enslaved population.

At various points in his life changes in attitude can be seen – as when he wrote a friend that when it became necessary to sell slaves he was determined to never break up families. Later when he was named Commander-in-Chief of the Continental Army he directed his Mount Vernon overseer to no longer buy nor sell any slaves. After the Revolutionary War he wrote to Robert Morris, "there is not a man living who wishes more sincerely than I do, to see a plan adopted for the abolition of it . . ." This same period saw a foreign visitor write regarding Washington's slaves that he dealt with them "far more humanely than his fellow citizens of Virginia." Further, after his presidency, his correspondence indicates a plan to use the moneys from the sale of his western lands to liberate his slaves. Though he never received what he thought was fair compensation for these lands, and no slaves were liberated during his lifetime, he later wrote a will stating that two years after his death the 123 slaves he owned outright were to be freed. Not only were they to be free but also funds from his estate were earmarked to support children, the sick, and the elderly. For slave children under the age of twenty-five, his will provided funds for teaching reading, writing, and a useful trade.

Many historians speculate that Washington's final decree was his attempt to be judged favorably by posterity – that the image of George Washington would thereby be consistent with the noble values of the Revolution. Less noble perhaps was the motivation provided by Virginia Quaker, Robert Pleasants, who liberated his slaves and tormented Washington by telling him that failure to liberate his own would leave an "everlasting stain on his reputation." Some speculation is that Lafayette's hostility to slavery was the overriding influence on Washington's change of views; others give credit to the realities of the unprofitability of sustaining a slave culture in Virginia. There is also the possibility that Washington's recognition of the successful small farms in New England peopled by free industrious men was proof that free men were more productive than those forced to work by threat of the lash.

Consequently there is unanimity that Washington's views on slavery certainly did change, but attempting to credit the evolution of Washington's thinking to any specific motivation is just speculative. Possibly there are many motivations and to attribute one more than another is just as speculative. Biographer Joseph J. Ellis suggests that Washington's conscience and self-interests were entangled in his own mind. Historian Ron Chernow concurs, saying that Washington had a "split personality" regarding slavery and abolition. Readers of the historical record are hard-pressed to say they fully understand Washington's motivations. We may record what was written and what was done, but cannot always accurately ascribe why these things were written and why they were done. To do so conjures a fiction – and with that said it is admitted that the following work is certainly one of speculative fiction.

A friend who reviewed one of my earlier books indicated that a book is successful if it accomplishes what the author intended. This advice sticks with me, so I have been forced to ponder just what I am trying to accomplish with this fictional memoir of William Lee. First, it seems like a good story – Washington's mulatto slave valet influences the values of Father of Our Country. It seemed an interesting premise that might be developed as a persuasive story. However, though I may write fiction it is not my main interest – exploring history is. So I must acknowledge that telling the complicated history of slavery during the founding days of our republic is my main goal. Along the way, as William Lee grows in his understanding of the wider world into which he is thrust, he tells his intriguing life's story. Of course, we would know nothing of his story without its relationship to the first president. Consequently, I hope the character of George Washington and the story of the American Revolution are presented in a readable and engaging manner.

As far as truth versus fiction, the events in Washington's life that are described – his life at Mount Vernon, his travels, battles, engagement with historical figures – are true to the historical record. Likewise the chronology of events is accurate. The fiction is the memoir itself – there is no memoir of William Lee. Consequently Washington's interactions with William Lee are all imagined. There are a few recorded documents that refer to William Lee. Those I have been able to find are noted at the conclusion of the memoir in Appendix 1.

Prologue

May 29, 1809

The fascination of the public with personalities involved in our colonial struggle with Great Britain for American independence has produced volumes of interviews and memoirs by and about the veterans of that great war – many of whom, being aged and in poor health are passing daily into eternity. One such veteran (even if perhaps an unwilling one), a man of nearly sixty years of age, has been hobbling about Mount Vernon Plantation as a curiosity ever since the death of his master ten years ago. "Billy Lee" with both legs crippled while in the service of his master, gained notoriety at the time of General Washington's death specifically because of the fact that he alone among the over 300 enslaved personages at that plantation was immediately freed by the will of the former president.

I first made Billy's acquaintance at the Battle of Brandywine in September of '77 where my regiment of light dragoons saw action. As horses were my business I noted with pleasure the care Billy took with his own mount as well as General Washington's. I complimented him on this and noted his fidelity to his work and to his master. I have since been made aware that this fidelity lasted through the revolution, and upon my circumstances now being near the nation's capital, I learned that Billy was still alive and living at Mount Vernon. Upon inquiry, I heard Billy described as a bit of a raconteur regarding his adventures with General Washington. Consequently, it arose in me the notion that his stories might be worth a more formal interview, and I was not disappointed.

I must first acknowledge that at Mount Vernon and throughout his service to the former president, the faithful servant was known simply as "Billy," and in speaking with General Washington's step-grandchildren they indicate this has long been the name that was used. However, this memoir is ascribed to him as William Lee for what I feel is a significant reason. When the former president died, his will gave his loyal valet not only his freedom, but for the first time it gave his name formal recognition – the will serving as a kind of certificate granting a full name. I have taken some liberty with this notion, as the related text of the President's will reads ". . . and to my Mulatto man William (calling himself William Lee) I give immediate freedom." So if we accept General Washington's bracketed words as they were most likely intended, "William Lee" is an alias. Our slaves are often not allowed the humanity of having a surname, but this narration never-the-less acknowledges that this is the story of William Lee.

As William Lee was General Washington's personal valet through the entire eight years of the war, and was with him night and day through every battle, every achievement, and every hardship endured, he witnessed history from a unique position. He alone saw the General each morning as he arose unadorned by the garments of rank; dressed and groomed him so he appeared the ultimate leader; cleaned the sweaty and dirty uniform at the end of day; and saw daily his master's sorrows, his anger, his frustrations, and even his tears. He likewise witnessed conversations between the General and subordinates, and between men of rank and state.

What is today remembered of the travails of those times, now some thirty years past? Is William Lee yet lucid enough to recall those times of strife? Are his recollections of interest to us today? Can we learn anything from this former slave? Now being a free man, what are his feelings about the institution of slavery? The revelations to these and sundry other questions will be made known in the following pages of this narration. Readers will be amazed at the memory exhibited and of the minute detail recalled. Moreover, his story will show the personal sacrifice and the subjugation of his own desires for the wellbeing of the Father of our Country. William's conscience and sense of morality may be surprising to many who do not acknowledge such qualities in a slave of African heritage. Furthermore his telling shows a remarkable understanding of the events that unfolded before his eyes, the ramifications of which far exceeded a simple relationship of slave to master.

I spoke with William Lee over a period of three weeks beginning in February of this year. He is a small mulatto man with black hair falling straight over his collar. He wears a red waistcoat and a cocked hat as if to emphasize his previous service. Each day we met in mid-morning in the small log cabin where he has resided as a free man these past ten years. He is crippled in both knees and frequently experienced jolting pain, but never-the-less welcomed someone to talk to, and as I was very interested in his story, we generally talked through the day. I have endeavored to take down his words as exactly as possible with sparse changes made only from the times he tended to repeat himself. The voice you hear as you read is his own – strong, intelligent, and forthright. I believe he has made no attempt to exaggerate his importance or significance in any matter, and I believe the following narrative is a true recollection of the time he spent with General Washington.

Colonel Elisha Sheldon (formerly of the 2nd Continental Light Dragoons)
Alexandria, Virginia
May 29, 1809

Journal of William Lee

Chapter 1

Back in them early days, when I was first brought here to Mount Vernon, when somebody shouted out, "the Colonel's a comin," everybody jumps. They says you'd best not be seen loafin' or leanin' when the Colonel was making his daily rounds. I hadn't been here long when I got a pretty good accounting of the man my master was and how he don't broke no foolishness. An old slave named Hector had near been trampled to death by a plow horse and recovered pretty good, but still has his busted arm in a sling. The colonel sees him standing in the garden watching the others hoe and rake, and grabs him by his good arm and lets out with a tongue-lashing. He picks up a rake with one hand and puts the other in his pocket and proceeds to rake up some hay. He says, "See I can rake just fine with one arm, why can't you? I'll bet you eat my food pretty good with one hand. If you can eat, by God, you can rake!"

Well, that was an early lesson that taught me to expect life at Mount Vernon would surely be about the same as most any plantation for a slave - work and obey from sun-up to sundown. That's all I seen my whole life. And the other slaves I met when I first get here said the Colonel was worse than most 'cause he kept a tight check on everything. They says he knows just how long every job should take, and if you take longer you'd better watch out. And if you says you was too sick to work, he kept track of how many days you missed and made you work even harder to make up lost time. Folks says he works them so hard 'cause he's always trying to do things new ways - says it's called scientific farming - and the Colonel gets real mad if you're not quick enough to learn the new ways.

But I have to tell you, I was luckier than most 'cause right away I get to do work I actually likes. I guess the part of my life's story you'd be most interested in began when I been on the place about two years and been situated to work in the stables and to groom the riding horses. It was a good job – I always liked horses – and it was sure a lot better than working all day in the fields. Well, you might imagine my surprise when one day out of the blue, the Colonel's valet, Syphax, comes up to me and says something like, "The Colonel has picked you out, boy. You better come with me!" I was standing in a stall wondering what I done wrong and thinking that I don't even know the Colonel ever much noticed me; maybe he'd seen me caring for his horses, but that's about all, and surely he'd never talked to me. The next thing I know I'm told I'm going to train to be the Colonel's valet! What? I could hardly believe what I was hearing! I'm going to be a valet – a house servant – and personal to the Colonel – I says to myself, "Oh my, oh my!"

This was in the spring of '70. I remember the year 'cause not only was I to have a new position, but also I was to travel with the Colonel – and soon. I was to go with him to Williamsburg. The Colonel was a delegate to the House of Burgesses and needed a valet to go with him. A course, in those days I didn't know Williamsburg from Africa. I was ignorant of city or country or anyplace other than maybe twenty miles around this here plantation.

As I said, I been the property of the Colonel for about two years, having belonged formerly to Mistress Mary Smith Ball Lee of Westmorland County. I was about sixteen years of age when purchased by the Colonel; though in truth none of us slaves ever knows our true age – so I'm just guessing. My brother Frank was a few years younger and he was sold along with me. I remember how scared he was to be going to a new place – so I had to pretend to be brave. Ever since I can remember Frank and me was always very close. Rumor was we had the same white father, but we never knew who that might be. Our mother never spoke of it – I guess she may have had some shame because if you is an attractive black woman on a plantation you never know who might take a fancy to you. So she spoke not at all about who our father might be – in fact she spoke very little about even her own people, so the only family we know is our mother. And I must also note that upon being torn from her bosom and sold to the Colonel, me and Frank never saw her again. I heard she died a few years after we left, but I never knew for sure.

Anyhow, I guess it was because I tended horses and colts at Mistress Lee's place, is why I got that good job over here. And they must have thought I was pretty good at it 'cause it was only after a few months that I was allowed to groom the Colonel's favorite horse named Chinkling – and I'd best have that fine horse groomed, saddled, and ready at a moment's notice, 'cause when the Colonel wanted to ride he wanted to ride now, and in those days his patience was short. So I was mighty surprised when Syphax, come to me and says I was to train for a valet. Syphax served the Colonel for many years, and tells me I'd best train up fast for this trip to Williamsburg.

I supposed Syphax was now too old to travel much and that was why a new valet was needed. But I knew nothing about such a position, and had great unease about how to do it. I was much relieved to learn that the master shaved himself each morning, as I had little experience with a razor. But I was soon to learn that it was still my duty to make sure the razor was properly set and stropped, and hot water ready for the Colonel's use. I also had to learn how to comb his hair. In those days he had reddish brown hair – and thick, too. People think the Colonel wore a wig – but I can tell you for a fact he never did. I learned to comb and pull his hair back just so – he called it a queue – then I powdered it, and tied a ribbon. No wig – only powder.

I had care of his clothes from that time until after the war. Unless he was particularly tired he usually dressed himself, but his coat and waistcoat had to be brushed and folded to his liking and placed on his chair. His body linen had to be clean. He also liked to dress with a fresh breeze in the room so I opened the window just a crack even later in the cold of

Valley Forge and Morristown. And he was keen about his boots; even after hard riding in rain or mud, he expected them clean and shining the next morning.

That first trip to Williamsburg was my first time traveling except when I was brought to Mount Vernon. I never seen a ferry before and there was one that took us and our horses across the Rappahannock River, but we had to ford every other river and stream between here and Williamsburg. The roads in them days was really just old Indian trails that had become wider over the years by all the riding back and forth. They was fair enough on dry days, but if you hit a big storm the roads got so muddy the wagons and carriages got stuck. We'd be drenched with dust or mud, and sometimes both when we stopped for the night.

It was on this first trip that I learned I was to stay close to the Colonel at all times. Most valets and other servants was bedded outside the taverns in stables or barns, but the Colonel says he don't want to have to hunt somebody up to fetch me when he wants something, and certainly don't want to have to come for me himself, so after I tended to the horses and cleaned our leggings and boots I usually slept in the hall outside his room or even against a side wall in his very room. Some of the other gentlemen complained, but I stayed close by, so I guess the Colonel don't lose no arguments.

Williamsburg was surely a place to see. I'd never seen a city. There was so much going on – so many people and houses, stores built on every corner, farmers coming in with loads of vegetables, oxen and mules pulling loads of lumber. One end of this big road sits a big red brick building they call the Capitol, where the burgesses meet, and down another road sits another fine brick building I hear is the governor's palace. Up the big road is more brick buildings they say is a college called William and Mary, named after some king and queen over in England. My eyes was wide with everything new to see.

I remember I see my first tin-smith, a silversmith too, and coopers – but most of all I remember all the other colored boys my age serving the important burgesses. Them boys had mostly been in Williamsburg before and teased this poor boy who only knew as much as any young slave boy raised on a farm. Most new to me was more white women than I'd ever seen in my life – all dressed in fancy wide skirts, skittering from one shop to another usually with their boys behind carrying boxes and parcels. And every place you looked somebody was making something interesting – oak barrels, tall shiny boots, muskets, fancy pottery, maps – more curiosities than I ever imagined.

Well, over the next few years, since the Colonel kept being elected as a burgess, we made more trips to Williamsburg and once to Richmond, so I got kind a use to being in a city and seeing how folks – white and black – lived in such a place. But most of the time we was here at Mount Vernon and my duties was confined to the mansion as valet and sometimes even as a butler. Two things stands out in my memory from those times – one was all the company we had to serve and entertain, and the second is when I met Onetta – but I'll tell you about her later.

You can't imagine how many people come to visit the Colonel and Mistress Washington. And I don't mean just drop in to say howdy-do. They stayed days – maybe weeks – and the work to make all those people happy – my word. All the washing, the fresh linens, all the meals, fetching supplies, serving on best china, keeping all the fires going, and us house servants running around all hours to makes folks comfortable. A course a lot of these folks was relatives – the Colonel had a mess of them, and it seemed to me they looked up to him, and I'm sure the Colonel was known as a wonderful host, but it sure made a lot of extra work for all us black folks.

And, for myself, the good thing about those times was Onetta. She was one of Mistress's seamstresses. And I might mention that many slave girls had this position.

Mistress called them her sewing circle – some might be cutting patterns, others spinning, young girls just learning to sew, and maybe a couple more knitting. Mistress was right there, too – sewing with the rest of them. A course it won't just sewing fancy stuff, although they did that too, but most of the time they was making clothes for all the slaves. Onetta caught my eye as I could tell she was Mistress's favorite – always gave her the finest sewing to do for white folks – and spoke to her most kindly. She'd always been one of Mistress Washington's slaves having been with her before she married the Colonel. I was quite smitten with her.

It wasn't too many months before we talked about getting married. I learn she come from a big family. In fact all of Onetta's family had been Custis slaves and they was now spread somewhere on one of the Colonel's many farms. A number of them worked the fields at the Dogue Run Farm. This was still part of Mount Vernon, but it had a different overseer, and its own slaves. When we get married, Onetta gets word out and everyone manages to come, and I has my brother Frank. We had a fine time jumping the broom and feasting on a special pig that Mistress Washington give Onetta as our wedding present. The Colonel don't give me nothing special and I don't suspect he would, but he was glad we got married. Even though slave marriages don't mean nothing under Virginia law, the Colonel always wants his slaves to marry someone on the plantation instead of meeting someone on some other farm and then having to sneak off to try to get together. If both husband and wife was from the same plantation all the children they had belonged to the master. It was the same then as now – the more slave children on a plantation means there'll be more adult slaves of value. That's just the way it is.

For me and Onetta married life was a bit different than for most all the other slave families. Most folks had Sundays off, and could do most anything they wanted to do, even leave the plantation if they has a pass. But I had to fit in my Sunday time with Onetta around the Colonel's schedule. After laying out his clothes and helping him with his toilet and dressing, I could slip away but only until he wants to go on a hunt or maybe visit somewhere, when a course I'd have to accompany him. And at night after attending to him, I had but a few hours in our quarters 'cause I was back in the morning when he Colonel gets up so I can start serving him all over again. But even if I don't have much time there, the quarters where us house servants lived was a sight better than most. Sad to say it's been tore down now to make way for that brick wing yonder on the north side of the mansion, but back then it was a two-story house we shared with three other families. It had a stone foundation, board floors, and four rooms with chimneys for each. We even had glazed windows, and believe me that was rare for slave quarters.

Chapter 2

I guess the most important part of my story really starts a year or so after we was married when I was told the Colonel would be taking another trip to Williamsburg. It was May of '74, and I recollect another rough trip 'cause of all the spring rains. We was drenched when we get to the city, but it was just in time to hear all the other burgesses in a stew over word that the British had just closed the port up in Boston. I later overheard some of the burgesses talking about what happened. Seems that when those white men dressed up like Indians and threw all that tea overboard it don't sit so good with the King over in England. He sends some ships and a whole bunch of soldiers and they just up and close the entire harbor. Said it was closed until they paid for all that tea and the mess they caused. No ships could come in and none could go out. The Colonel and the others know this would kill the city 'cause it depended mightily on trade with England and the other colonies. So they met every day in the Capitol building and talk about what they should do.

As for me, after I tend to the morning chores and the horses I don't have much to do better than get with the other valets and laugh and trade stories. We knows better than get into any loud mischief so we just hang around outside and remind each other not to make too much fuss or we'd end up in a bad fix. Well, this one valet says he was a free man and could just leave any time he had a mind to. He talks big 'cause the rest of us is slaves. So I asks what was like to be free. It was the first time I chanced to meet a black man who was free, and I wondered what did he do? How was it different from being a slave? He was doing the same things I was. We was all expected to be loyal, to be clean, to be ready to serve whenever needed. He says he got paid and could leave whenever he wants. I asks why don't he just go, and he grins – said he knows he has it pretty good.

About this time I learn how other people think of the Colonel. I had heard from ol' Syphax that the Colonel was an important man, but when I see other white men in his company I really understood. First of all, my master was a big man. He always stood about a half a head taller than most any other man in the room and he was 'specially stout in the hips. Second, he was respected because he been the head of the colonial Virginia militia during the war with the French, and I later learned he been famous for this even in England. And he was also well known for his strength. One day Mr. William Byrd gets the Colonel in a bet with a bunch of other delegates. He bets that the Colonel can crush a walnut between just his thumb and forefinger. We was all peeking in the window and watching as he did it with ease. The other men had to pay up on their bets. I was sure proud to be the Colonel's boy that day.

I met some other important men then, too. Mr. Jefferson was young, almost as tall as the Colonel but very skinny, and don't say much. And Mr. Patrick Henry we could always hear talking even when they closed the windows to try to be secret. He was about the loudest and most talkative man I ever did hear. One man, kind of quiet, but I remember well, was Mr. George Wythe. Seemed like everyone looked up to him for advice.

I recollect the day the delegates was removed from the Capitol building by Governor Dunmore. He says they not suppose to be talking against the King and saying he had no right to close that Boston port. Then we see through the window this man dressed in a fancy robe come in banging this big staff on the floor. We can't exactly hear what he says, but what happened was the burgesses had to leave the Capitol right then and there. It don't matter much though cause they meet at Raleigh Tavern just up the street. It was easier for me to hear what they was talking about in the tavern 'cause no one seems to care if it was secret no more. The gist of all the talk was electing people to go to Philadelphia and have this big meeting with people from the other colonies. The Colonel was one of the main ones talking against the King so I won't surprised he was one of those chosen to go. I don't know it at the time, but them calling for that Philadelphia meeting would soon shape the rest of my life.

As we rode back to Mount Vernon the Colonel says I would be going with him, but that we had a few months before we had to go. I started thinking that I would just be getting back to Onetta and then have to leave again. While I was feeling sad thinking about this the Colonel surprises me with some casual talk as we was riding along. It was the first time he spoke to me not as just his servant but almost man to man. I never know him to do this with any of his servants, so I was more than a mite surprised. But you spends a lot of time side by side on a lonely roadway with nothing to break the monotony beside the steady drum of hoof beats. As we ride, I was always alert for commands – maybe to ride ahead and find a better place to cross a stream, or seek out a tavern where we might stop, or do whatever else the Colonel wants. But this trip as we rode, the Colonel starts in asking me questions – especially about how come I learned to ride so good. I tell him Mistress Lee always wanted a boy to ride with her and I had been trained for that purpose when I was young, and was taught to be a pretty good horseman. But when she got sick she don't ride no more, and I always supposed that was why she decided I won't good for much else and sold me to the Colonel.

We talked about horses some, and the Colonel asks what I think of Chinkling. Well, I'd been grooming him for years, and seen how fine the Colonel looked riding him, and I tells him I thought Chinkling was a mighty fine horse. Then to my surprise, he says to me, "Well, suppose you try him out." A course that was fine with me, so we switched horses, and the Colonel says I rides him very well. I still don't know what he had in mind and knows it won't my place to ask, and it won't until the next day when we neared Mount Vernon that he says, "I think Chinkling will be your horse from now on."

I was struck dumb by this, as he had always been the Colonel's favorite, but he then tells me I would need such a horse if I was to be his new huntsman. His huntsman! Oh my!

When I come to this place I could barely tell a hound from a fox. And now I'm to be his huntsman! I don't know what to say. The Colonel says he has another horse in mind for himself especially for foxhunting, a half-Arabian stallion by the name of Blueskin. Turns out Blueskin was a beautiful mostly white stallion about seventeen hands. He tells me he got him from the Sultan of Morocco – which a course was the first time I had ever hear of such a person or place.

My new position as huntsman on top of being valet gives me considerable standing with the other slaves. While there was always envy of us house servants, I never found it hard to handle long as I don't try to act big, or put nobody down. I realizes status was okay if you was white. White folks always seem to look up to people they consider their betters. But if you is black and act uppity, no one likes you – white or black. I knows I was mighty lucky to be where I was, so I paid attention to my duties and keep my mouth shut. With that said, I believe the Colonel was a fair master. Not that I mean no one was ever punished – the lash was always a threat. The thing was, the colonel had this system where before a slave was punished he got to tell his side of the story. When an overseer wants to punish a slave he has to take the complaint to the Colonel – and even later when we was on some battlefield in Lord knows where, the overseer has to justify his punishment in a letter to the Colonel. The main thing with the Colonel, and I suspect with most white folks who owns slaves, is that the punishment is supposed to change the way a slave behaves. I recollect two, maybe three times that some poor boy don't change enough to suit the Colonel and was sold to a buyer from the West Indies. I suppose this was a lesson of what could happen for the rest of us.

But the Colonel also tried to reward people who worked hard – sometimes with extra clothes or blankets, or a pot for cooking. As I see it over my long life, what the good masters want most is obedience – but not out of fear – rather loyalty. They sees it like this – I gives you food, shelter, and clothes – and you gives me work. Maybe it's tough that you is a slave and my property, but that's just the way the world is. They wants to be seen as good masters – and I suppose this makes them feel good about themselves.

Well anyway, it was to be several months before we left for Philadelphia, and many of those days we did indeed spend chasing the foxes. I was a sight to see – bright red hunting jacket, black cap, and this French horn I had to use to signal the hounds. Took me a few weeks to learn all the different signals, but I got pretty good at it. I had but one order and that was to keep up with the hounds, and with Chinkling I could do it. We'd take off through brake and tangled wood, and I'd seldom even needed to spur him on. Chinkling was a great leaper and I rode low in the saddle. My, what a fine time we had.

But it won't all chasing foxes. The Colonel has four farms to check on and he did it most days. We'd start early in the morning and ride out – sometimes first to check on his orchards and then ride to the wheat fields, or to see the corn. Then maybe we'd go next to see how the sheep was doing – at one time he had hundreds of them – and a slave named Nero looked after them with his whole family – including his wife and children, with no white overseer nowhere in sight. Then we might go to check on the mules. I heard it said the Colonel was the first to raise mules in Virginia. Some said they was smarter than horses, but I never had time to find this out for myself.

About once each week we'd ride over to the gristmill on Dogue Creek. My brother Frank was one of the laborers there sometimes, and I always looked for him. Later he became a kind of apprentice to Mr. Evans the miller who came over from England just to build and run the Colonel's mill. It looked to me like it pretty much ran itself with all that water keeping the wheel turning, but I never really understood how everything inside worked – a bunch of turning wheels and big oak gears smashing together like that. But Frank knows everything about how it all works and liked to show me what he knew.

Sometimes I'd be sent to fetch someone the Colonel wanted to question. Once, the boys in the fishery was working by themselves, and the Colonel don't see the overseer, Mr. Hastings, anywhere about, so I'm told to ride high and low along the waterfront until I find him. The fishery was a big place; I suspect the Colonel made a lot of money selling all them herring. There was maybe ten boys spent all day salting fish and a bunch more working in the smokehouse. The Colonel told Hastings before that he wanted them boys watched that they won't stealing fish, and with Hastings not there he wanted to know who was doing the watching. When Hastings followed me back to the Colonel it just took a few sharp words to straighten out that poor white man – not that I felt sorry for him, cause to be truthful, I don't mind seeing an overseer get a dressing down. And I do recall that ol' Hastings was on the job every time we come by after that.

Oh, and we also has to go and check on the distillery. The Colonel made some fine corn whisky – at least that was how the story went – as none of us slaves had better ever be caught sampling it.

It was a busy time for the Colonel – which meant a busy time for me, too. Many days we went to Alexandria City where the Colonel was trying to raise up some men for a militia. The Colonel wore his old uniform from back in that war with the French – it must have been about fifteen years old, but to me it looked just fine. Once I overheard him talking about how unfit these white men was to be soldiers – said they come from the lower classes, don't have no discipline, and was so poor they only has the clothes on their backs. He was always writing letters and such complaining that if those burgesses in Williamsburg wanted Virginia to have militia they has to come up with money to equip the men. Hardly none of them has muskets neither – they did their training with broomsticks. Well, he finally gets up about a hundred men and taught them to march and obey commands, but I never did hear if they got muskets. I heard the Colonel complain that they should get some pay too – but I don't think they ever did.

Those militiamen maybe don't dress like soldiers, but the Colonel don't want to appear in nothing other than his finest. He decides his old uniform won't much do no more and while we was in Alexandria he has another whole uniform made – and it was indeed a sight. The coat was dark blue turned up with gold-like buttons, buff waistcoat and breeches and white stockings, complete with fancy gold lace epaulettes with fringe. This was to be his dress uniform and I was to be sure it was well packed, and also I had to include this kind of necklace that showed his important rank, and a purple sash and a dandy white plume too.

Back here at Mount Vernon the Colonel says there was no time any more for special hunt days. He was so busy he kind of combined his hunt with checking on the farms. We was out riding maybe twelve hours those days. The Colonel may have felt he was rushed and all, but I thought it was not a bad job for a young buck slave like me out riding all day – and I got to ride one of the best horses on the plantation. I knows I ride pretty good or I wouldn't have been made huntsman. A course I don't present a striking figure like the Colonel. He was a pleasure to watch sitting up straight full stride on Blueskin. And one reason he looked so good was the Colonel wants his riding clothes to be just as fit as his military uniform. He likes this blue riding frock and a fancy scarlet waistcoat threaded with gold lace, and always wore a black velvet cap and high black boots. Yes indeed, he was mighty striking. In fact, I once did hear even such a good horseman as Mr. Jefferson speak of the Colonel as the "best horseman of his age, and the most graceful figure that could be seen on horseback." Pretty good praise! I don't know it then, but it was a good thing we could both ride like we did, 'cause in a few years we'd be outracing British musket balls.

Chapter 3

By the time me and the Colonel has to leave for Philadelphia, me and Onetta has us a one-year-old son we named Isaac. He was just beginning to walk, and laughed each time he fell over and got back up on his chubby little legs. I hated to leave my new family, but a slave don't have no say about such things. We get pretty used to just doing what we is told. But I was worried 'bout how long we'd be gone. Philadelphia was said to be about an eight-day's ride, and the Colonel says we might be there for many weeks, so it would be a while before we would be home. I had no idea when I would again see Onetta and my little Isaac.

There was a lot the Colonel has to do before leaving. His cousin, Lund Washington, was to be in charge and they took several days riding around together and talking about things. I was busy packing, and saying my goodbyes. As it turned out this trip was not to be just the Colonel and me. A few days afore we was to leave, Mr. Henry and Mr. Edmund Pendleton, another of the burgesses, arrived at Mount Vernon. They was to journey with us. I was glad to have the company as each gentleman had his valet with him, so I knows we will have a bit of fun at night after the requirement of our services.

It was mid September when we begin our trip. The Colonel likes to get an early start when he travels, and we'd stop mid-morning at a tavern for breakfast, and again for a meal in the afternoon. As it was still pretty hot, the gentlemen all agreed to travel near 'til dark, as that was the coolest part of the day. In those days traveling through Maryland and Pennsylvania the folks in those places don't know who the Colonel or any of the gentlemen was, so no one has to answer a lot of questions when we meet folks along our way. In later years whenever anyone saw the Colonel coming by they'd commence to "hurrah" and join right in with us so that by the time we rode into town there'd be a parade.

On this trip the Colonel gets the others to lodge in taverns run by all kinds of different people. Even then I guess he was thinking kind of political like. Maybe he believed the more folks he visited the more he'd find out about how they felt about the British taxes and such. I'm not for certain if it was this trip or others, but in Pennsylvania I recall meeting Scots and Swedes and I believe we lodged with Germans and Quakers – even with Indians. The Colonel was no stranger to several Indian languages, as back in that war with the French he had many different Indian guides and allies. He seemed to have a lot of respect for most red men, although many times I hear him say they was dirty. I was kind of puzzled that he could think both ways about them.

In Maryland we stopped at several inns run by Catholics, which surprised me, as in Williamsburg I heard many a Virginia gentleman sneer at their mention. I don't believe Mr. Henry and Mr. Pendleton were as much at ease with Catholics as the Colonel was. He seemed to think they was as good as anybody else.

As we got closer to Philadelphia the roads was wider and better kept. The Colonel grumbled that he had never been able to get the other burgesses to do more taxes for money to improve roads in Virginia. He called them shortsighted. In years after, I did observe that in all our travels, the further north we went the better roads we traveled on.

Philadelphia was everything the Colonel told me it would be. He said there was more people there than any other city in North America including Boston and New York. It was near dark as we entered the city, but much to my amazement the streets was lit like it was almost daylight. They had flames burning inside these glass lanterns up on tall poles – and they was set all over the city and burned a lot brighter than candles. They was pretty too, and someone said they burned whale oil, and it seemed a mighty good idea. The Colonel was looking for a building called Carpenter's Hall. It turned out to be easy to find as it was a brand new brick building just up the street from where a man lived that the

Colonel said he very much wanted to see – Dr. Benjamin Franklin – as he was an old friend of the Colonel's from back in the war with the French. We found out that Dr. Franklin was still in London, but years later I was to meet him and even had a conversation with him.

Philadelphia was very crowded so the gentlemen had some worry over where they would find room and board. I knew these white men would eventually find something, and further they would not concern themselves about accommodations for us servants. We would take whatever we got, and say nothing. But as it turned out they found a boarding house that even provided breakfast and dinner for us servants on a rear porch.

Each morning the delegates to this First Continental Congress, as they called it, assembled at this Carpenter's Hall, and after our usual morning services for our masters, we had pretty much the next few days to ourselves as the Congress met most of the day and we valets were not needed until the dinner hour. My new friends quickly found card and dice games in alleys and behind most every tavern, and tried to get me to join them. Ol' Syphax had warned me about these kinds of games and told me to steer clear of them. He knew I had a bit of pocket change from all the tips I made from folks who enjoyed our many foxhunts, but I wouldn't have gambled away any of it even if I'd not been warned. What I mainly wanted to do was find out about that busy city, especially about all of the colored people who was running in and out of shops and houses, riding horses and driving teams – 'cause they seemed to be pretty much on their own.

I never seen a riverfront city before, and the busiest place of all was right at the docks, and they stretched for what seemed like miles. Everywhere I looked there was something going on with shipbuilding. There must have been twenty or thirty yards where I could see poplar masts sticking up like tall trees. I was amazed at how maybe ten or twelve men could move them around and use these long ropes to raise them up. In another yard I seen a lot more men was cutting and planing long wide boards. I asked what they was for and was told they was for making the hull of a ship. I asked, "What's a hull?" and this old black man tells me they was for the keel of a ship, but he looks at me like I was pretty dumb for not knowing what a hull was, so I don't ask what a keel was.

In some ways these shipyards was like a busy plantation, but the jobs people was doing was different. I never seen tar before, but on the waterfront there'd be big vats of it over a fire with men constantly stirring. I seen blacksmith shops before, but in Philadelphia they had what they called iron forges where they made big things out of iron – like ship's anchors.

But the waterfront was more than just building ships – it was loading and unloading them too. Seemed like there was no end to men walking these ramps from the docks to the ships carrying everything I could imagine – barrels of nails, long pieces of lumber, bags of wheat, flour, or molasses, bushel baskets of fish – everything. And there was navy type ships too. I don't know what they was called when I first seen them, but many was gunboats and frigates with three and even four masts, and sailors leaning over and hollering at the boys loading and unloading.

And it won't just right at the docks where I seen all these new sights but also across the road. It was just lined with taverns – more than I ever seen – and men and women drinking and laughing – and right in the middle of the day. But churches was there, too, and houses and shops – workmen of all types – white men and black – some busy as beavers and others kind of just lazing about.

I suspected with all these tall ships and busy shipyards that many high and mighty people must live in this city. But the only folks I could see was just the working people, and I noted that they was both white and black. And I could plainly see the whites was shopkeepers and doing the mostly skilled work and the blacks was doing the hard labor jobs. I'd heard lots of colored were free in Philadelphia, but by just watching them work I couldn't tell who was slaves and who might be free – but it got me to thinking – whether they be free or not, it's really just like back at Mount Vernon where blacks did all the hard labor. And the more I thought about it, I says to myself, "Yup, that's just the way the world is."

I was learning a lot from what I seen in Philadelphia, but one job particularly caught my eye 'cause just as many whites as blacks was doing it. At first I had no idea what they was doing. They was working on ships that had been pulled up on land, and they was sitting on benches suspended by ropes from the sides of the ships. As I got closer I could see they was filling cracks between the boards with what looked like black rope. They had chisels and hammers, and was pounding the rope between the cracks. I watched for some time and one of the black men saw me standing there and called out asking if I was looking for work. I told him, no, I was just looking to see what they was all doing. He stopped what he was doing and came down to talk with me.

"You're not from around here, are you?" he asked. I told him I was from a plantation in Virginia and had never before seen a shipyard. This man don't look at me like the other man I asked a question who made me feel stupid, so I asked about his work. He said it was called caulking, and had to be done between each plank throughout the ship. He said on a new ship the wooden planks would swell when the ship was first launched, and this made a pretty tight seal, but as the boards aged they would shrink so they needed caulk between each plank. He told me the caulk they used was made from hemp soaked in tar, and was called oakum. This oakum had to be placed carefully in each crack and then set in place using a hammer and chisel. I said it seemed like slow work, and he said it was, and that's why he had to keep at it 'cause caulkers was paid by how many feet they did each day. With that said he went back to his work. But I was still curious to learn more and so I just stayed there watching.

Before too long all the men stopped working and come off their boards for the midday meal. I walk over to the man who talked to me and made his acquaintance.

He says he calls himself Ned Baxter, but for his early life his only name was Ned. He was a talkative fellow and told me he worked on a farm back in Delaware ever since childhood, and did whatever work he was told to do just like all the other slaves. He said when he was about twelve he was put with a white carpenter as a helper – kind of an apprentice – and after a few years he was good enough so he could make simple chairs, beds, barrels and other stuff on his own. He said he had a good man for a master who let him keep most of the money from selling things he made himself as long as he made them on his own time. Said it wasn't much money at first, but he sees if he saves it and don't spend it on trinkets and stuff like the other slaves who gets tips, he might end up with quite a bit. I remember how proud he sounded when he said, "So I worked double time for maybe five years and you know what – I had money enough to buy myself free!"

Well, this really sparked my curiosity 'cause I wanted to learn more about how it was to be free. I asked if all the colored men caulking was free like him, and he says maybe half was free and half was slaves. So I says well how does this work out for getting paid. He said he was paid one pence for every twenty feet he caulked, and that many days he did as many 240 feet. As at this time I had no knowledge of arithmetic, I asked how much money this was, and he replied it was 12-pence which was the same as one shilling. Since the Colonel many times in Williamsburg gave me coins to pay for meals and supplies, I had some sense of money and what it was worth, but I don't know if Philadelphia money was the same. And I was still curious about the men who was slaves, and I asked, "So they gets paid, too?"

Ned laughs at this and says, "Well, yes and no." A course this puzzles me and Ned goes on to explain that yes they do gets paid, but has to give all the money to their masters. A good master might give a few pence as a kind of reward if the slave makes him a lot of money, but mostly the masters keep it all.

Ned had to get back to work, and I had to return to serve the Colonel, but all that night I thought about Ned. He said he was free and got to keep his money, but there was slaves who did the same work, too. So I kept wondering how was Ned's life different from a slave's. I determined to go back and talk to him, and the next day I was at the dock again when the men stopped at midday. The first thing I asked Ned about was 'cause he said his name was Ned Baxter, and I wanted to know how he got that Baxter name. He said he would never have come to Philadelphia except for this white farmer he only knew as Mr. Baxter. He bought a lot of chairs and other stuff from Ned over the years and took a liking to him. He told Ned about Philadelphia where lots of colored men was free, and he'd best go there to have a better life. So when Ned gets his free papers he has them write Ned Baxter as his name, and that was his name ever since.

When he arrived in Philadelphia he don't have enough money to buy carpenter's tools so he takes a job as a laborer on the docks. He says he could barely live on the low wages they paid and often had to sleep out of doors on the cold ground – so being free weren't looking too good. So he looked for other work. A lot of blacks was caulkers, but this too required tools 'cause different chisels was needed depending on the size of the cracks to be filled. It took him most a year to save enough money for his tools, but now he had been at it for three years and liked it just fine. "The boss man ain't so bad in this line of work," he told me. "Since everybody does piece work, you only get paid for whats you do, so unless you're really slow or sloppy with your work, he don't say much." It seemed that even slave caulkers had reason to work fast if their masters sometimes let them keep some of the money.

I went back each mid-day when I had no duties, and talked to Ned. I wanted to know about this freedom business and how he lived with the money he made. I asked him, "Okay, you say you make twelve pence every day. How do you live on this? What do things cost?" He runs down how he spends his money: Supper of cheese and beer was three pence, a small loaf of bread was one pence, a pound of butter was ten pence, a pound of cheese six pence – and he went on and on telling me how much everything cost. I couldn't keep up with it all but it made me think about my own life. At Mount Vernon, me and Onetta don't know the cost of nothing, and never much thought about it. By being free and earning money, Ned had to buy everything and keep track of whether he had enough. Was Ned's life better than mine? If so, how? He said he was happy with his life, and being free made him feel more like a man – said he could go where he wanted and when he wanted. He had a wife named Francie – she was free too, and they was expecting a child. Their home was in a basement under a livery, pretty small and don't always smell so fine, and it cost ten shillings each month, which he thought was too much for what it was, but it would do until they could find another place. This made me think of my situation. I don't have no choice about leaving Onetta and Isaac, but on the other hand I never worry about where I would sleep as the Colonel always decides that, and I never worry about enough to eat.

So as I thought about it, I knew I was luckier than most slaves. I liked my master and mostly got to do things I liked. But there in Philadelphia I got a taste of being on my own time. I got a feeling I understood what Ned was talking about – it won't so much that the work he did was different from a slave doing the same thing – it was 'cause as a free man Ned got to decide what to do for himself – and slaves never gets to decide nothing.

At Mount Vernon all of us did what we was told and did it the way we had been taught. Only the bad ones disobeyed. It was to my great advantage to be good – to stay in the Colonel's good graces. It seemed that freedom was more complicated. Ned's Francie worked daily for a woman she cooked and cleaned for, and I guess got paid some, but together the best they could do was live in a basement with a dirt floor. It don't sound so good. While whites might always call me "boy," in my own head I never felt less than a man – perhaps not as good a man as my master – but still a man. But Ned got me thinking about what it might feel like not to be owned by somebody, and maybe I couldn't understand this 'cause a the trust the Colonel had in me that gave me a kind of freedom.

It was talking with Ned that got me thinking so much about my life as a slave. If I was free, how would I get money? After paying for food every day, Ned and Francie still had to pay just to stay in that basement house, and what if they had to buy shoes or a blanket. How many pence or shillings would they cost? Once a year the Colonel always made sure that each slave household got new clothes and a new blanket, and got a monthly allowance of pork or fish and corn meal. Even the folks working on the farms had a cabin to sleep in – most with the same dirt floors as Ned's place, and certainly no glazed windows, but they don't have to find a place themselves. Was Ned really better off? I went back to the service of the Colonel each evening wondering about these things.

Chapter 4

I get back to Carpenter's Hall one day just in time to overhear that loud talking Mr. Henry say something about the Colonel. He says, "Colonel Washington has the soundest of judgment and is the greatest man on the floor." I thought this was a mighty fine thing to say. Another day when they come out of the building they was all still talking and waving their arms, so I figure it must be 'bout something important. I overhear the Colonel, Mr. Henry, and Mr. Pendleton saying that the delegates agreed to what they called a non-importation of British goods until the Redcoats stopped treating Boston so bad. They said the colonies won't buy nothing from England while they did intolerable things. I won't sure I understood the big words and everything, but some of the other valets was listening too, and some say it means if English merchants can't sell their stuff in the colonies, they'll go broke, and so they'll tell the King to get off the backs of those folks in Boston, and open the port back up. I asks the Colonel 'bout this and he says I heard right, and says the delegates also sent a big letter to the King saying he should treat the colonies better. But I don't think those delegates really thinks the King is going to listen, 'cause I hear they voted to meet again in Philadelphia in about six months.

Me and the Colonel traveled home, just the two of us, as Mr. Henry and Mr. Pendleton stayed a while longer in the city. The Colonel seemed as anxious to get back to Mount Vernon as I was. I guess he missed his wife, too. I know I sure missed my Onetta. As we traveled, I don't know if the Colonel thought it proper to have another conversation with me, but there was something Ned told me I really wanted to know more about, so I thought I'd ask the Colonel. I told him I heard tell of a Quaker school that some of the colored children went to in Philadelphia. Did he know about that? He reckoned that he had heard about it – but don't offer to say no more – so I thought it best to keep quiet.

It was getting on in October as we traveled, and there was a chill in the air. Before long we was in the middle of an early season snowfall. The Colonel's new favorite horse, Blueskin, has never seen snow before and become skittish, especially as the snow begins to pile up. It was up to 'bout his fetlock when Blueskin just stops walking. We tried tying a line from Chinkling and just sort of pulling Blueskin along, but he won't be pulled. Ended up with me getting off my horse and cajoling Blueskin as I held his harness and walked beside him. We must a walked three hours in the snow like that until we come to a tavern where we waited out the storm until the next morning.

As we traveled, I was still thinking about the day before. I don't mind the walking and the tugging even if I was wet and cold – just figured it was my job – but it occurs to me for the first time it was more than just my job or my duty – it was my place. I knew my place. All of us slaves knows our place. It was when you don't know your place – and stay in it – that you gets in trouble. Trying to talk about a school for colored children was out of place.

When we gets back to Mount Vernon one of the first things the Colonel does is write letters to his friends telling them he was looking for another horse. Blueskin continued to be his favorite for hunting, but shortly the Colonel receives a fine horse from his friend Thomas Nelson. Come to like him so much he even names that horse Nelson. It was tall, well over sixteen hands, a handsome chestnut in color with white face and legs. This horse won't skittish about nothing and become the Colonel's favorite throughout the war – in fact he learned to stand as still as a statue even under the roar of cannon fire – while I'm sometimes shaking in my boots!

On the plantation, the Colonel's not only concerned with his horses, but with all's going on with his farms. I ride with him so I see what he tells folks to do, but my concern is for my own little family. Isaac has grown so much I hardly know him, and I guess he feels that way about me, too, as he shies from me at first until I holds him and sing his favorite tunes. The Colonel gave me a bit more time to spend with him, and I surely was glad.

While we was gone, Mistress Washington had kept Onetta busy with sewing baby clothes for her new daughter-in-law whose marriage to her son Jacky Custis had been earlier in the year. Jacky always treated me fine – though he was a mite strict with his own personal slaves, probably cause Mistress had always tended to treat the boy like a little prince, and the Colonel kinda had to go along with this.

Onetta made a big set of clothes and blankets for Jacky and his new bride even though the baby had not yet been born. She was so busy sewing that Isaac had to be cared for by Onetta's grandmother. This was fine with us and right typical on a slave plantation, 'cause when older women was no longer useful in the fields they was always put to raising the slave children. Our quarters was now more crowded, but squeezing more people into a slave's quarters was just the way life was. I knew we was still luckier than most and was reminded of it by Onetta's father's situation. He tended the apple orchards and cider mill, and along with seven other men was cramped into one small log cabin over at the River Farm. He barely found room enough to place his mattress on the dirt floor.

I'd been pondering this whole slavery thing ever since my days spent talking with Ned Baxter. Ned give me a sense of the money it took to live as a free person, and I could see that with a wife and child it required a fair sum. So I begin wondering how much it cost to keep a slave family on a plantation like Mount Vernon. Me and Onetta and Isaac lived better than Ned; I was sure we ate better, and had better clothes. How much did this cost? I wondered if men like the Colonel had to figure this stuff out. He had lots of families like us to feed and clothe, and provide houses for; so how much did it all cost? He has maybe a hundred slaves growing wheat and corn and such, but how much money does he get when he sells these crops? And there was about fourteen household slaves like Onetta and me who don't provide any income for the farm, and there was a bunch of folks like Onetta's grandmother who was too old to work – but still ate and wore clothes. I began to wonder if this slavery business really made any money for people like the Colonel.

Chapter 5

Well, life at Mount Vernon went on like before. I rode with the Colonel and his friends on the hunt, strangers came and went from the plantation, and Isaac got bigger and into more mischief with each step he learned to take. The Colonel seemed more anxious than ever to hunt most every day. I don't know it then, but I come to think he probably guessed he might shortly be gone from this place for quite a spell and wanted to get in all the hunting he could. There was two hunts during this time that stands out in my memory. One was 'cause I got the Colonel to change his mind about something. We'd been out all day hunting after a black fox. Now black foxes is rare and we ran the hounds all day and into the twilight never catching that devil. The horses was 'bout dead and the hounds, too. I pleaded that we never again chase such a fox – only sticking to gray ones – and much to my pleasure and surprise, the Colonel agreed.

The other hunt stands out 'cause I thought one of us might get shot. The Colonel never did truck with poachers on his property. All the overseers had strict instructions to shoo off any one likely poaching and let the Colonel know right away who they might be. Well one day we was out hunting near Dogue Run and we see this poacher dragging some mallards he's just shot and is proceeding to put in his canoe. Well, the Colonel takes off like a shot a hollering at this man who then proceeds to raise his musket and aim it at the Colonel. Well, the Colonel just spurs Blueskin right up on the man, then leaps off, grabs the canoe and proceeds to jerk the musket out of the man's hand before you can say, "yahoo." Then he grabs the man by the collar and flails away at him. That was a hunt I'll never forget, and that poor poacher won't either!

Sometime in early spring, the days of hunting was over. The Colonel has to go back to Williamsburg and a course I go with him. We take a different road this time as we stopped off to see Jacky and his new bride at the White House plantation on the Pamunkey River in New Kent County. The

Colonel has raised Jacky from the age of four, and I suspect was a good stepfather; but I use to think he shouldn't always be giving the boy everything he wants. I'd not met his new wife, Miss Eleanor, who they called Nellie, but she was mighty pleased to receive the fine baby clothes my Onetta made for her, and I was proud to hear her say so. We stayed overnight and then went on to Williamsburg where the burgesses commenced their days of talking. A course, the Colonel, as I suspected would happen, was again chose to go to Philadelphia for the Second Continental Congress.

Just a few days before we was to return to Mount Vernon and then head on to Philadelphia, we almost get ourselves involved in a battle before that Revolutionary War even started. The Colonel had retired to his rooms at Chowning's Tavern and I just finished my last chores and was ready for bed myself, when I hear such a commotion from further up on Duke of Gloucester Street. People was yelling and screaming, "They've stolen the powder; they've stolen the powder!" Well, I don't know what powder they was talking about, but I run up the street to where by now there must be a hundred people. They was screaming about the gunpowder that was kept in the city's magazine. The story was a troop of Redcoat sailors had been ordered by Governor Dunmore to take the gunpowder aboard a ship 'cause he was afraid some of the hot heads might use it against him. From the anger I saw that night, I suppose Dunmore was right to be worried. It seemed to me that all the white men in Williamsburg was ready to go home and get their muskets to go after the sailors.

Just about then the Colonel and some other burgesses show up and talk to the crowd. It takes a while but things settle down. They talk about what to do all the rest of the night, and it was decided that a bunch of burgesses would simply go see Governor Dunmore and tell him the gunpowder won't his and won't the King's either and that they wanted it back. Dunmore won't going to back down, but then Mr. Henry arrives with about five hundred Culpeper militia and the Governor decides he best change his mind. Problem was, the gunpowder was long gone – but the Colonel goes right up and tells Dunmore the gunpowder was worth 330 pounds – and to everyone's surprise Dunmore paid it right then and there! And shortly after that the governor decides he'd best skedaddle, and he takes his family aboard a British ship and never returns to Williamsburg.

After all that excitement, we spent a few days on the road back to Mount Vernon, but we was barely there long enough to say our goodbyes and then we was to be off again for Philadelphia. I overheard the Colonel tell Mistress he'd be home as soon as possible from this Second Continental Congress, but I had a sense that this time we might be gone a spell longer and I held my Onetta and Isaac quite a bit tighter. I knew they would be all right as Mistress Washington had always been kindly toward Onetta, but I still left with more than a few tears in my eyes.

The Colonel made sure I packed his two military uniforms just so – as he planned to wear the new one each day to the Congress. We had fine May weather and that was a good thing because for this trip the Colonel decides to ride in his new custom-made coach with Giles doin' the driving. I was glad not to be the only servant from Mount Vernon and have someone I knew goin' with us.

I was guessing that trying to be unnoticed was not the Colonel's way any longer. I followed behind on Chinkling and leading both Nelson and Blueskin. We make it to Philadelphia in just five days, and people there sure take notice of this fancy rig that brought the Colonel to the city. It just added to the general excitement that I figured must have to do with what these delegates to the Congress might decide.

We just got settled into our quarters when another ruckus breaks out. It seems we got there just in time for the biggest welcome celebration I ever seen. Church bells was ringing all over the city and hundreds of folks was marching down to the piers. A ship from England just docked and everyone was there to welcome Benjamin Franklin back to America. Folks said he had spent years trying to get England to back off with their taxes and stuff so there won't be no war. The Colonel goes to say hello and do too, but I reckoned Dr. Franklin must not have had much success with that King or else why would they be having this here Second Congress?

Well, this time the Congress meets at the Pennsylvania State House that was bigger than Carpenter's Hall. Most of the men I don't know, but I recognized the ones from Virginia like Mr. Jefferson, Mr. Henry, and Mr. Wythe. They had a lot to talk about because not only had violence almost happened with the gunpowder in Williamsburg, but it had happened for a fact just two days earlier up in Massachusetts at some place called Concord, when British and local militia had a battle and men was killed on both sides. The Congress argued if they should do anything about this. Turned out they talked for days – guess they couldn't figure if they should do something or not. So since I don't have much to do most days I went to look for my friend Ned.

I found him doing the same old thing – sitting on his scaffold board caulking between planks. He was glad to see me and we talked some about the stuff the white folks was so excited about. He was excited too, because he and Francie had moved from their basement under the livery, and rented a small house near the piers. She had her baby, and their new place don't smell from horses, and had a board floor and two windows. Best of all, the house was in a small community of other free blacks and they had neighbors a lot like them. He said they called themselves Methodists because some preacher in England had written some business about all black folks having the right to live free. Ned said he don't know much about it but his neighbors all went to the church so he and Francie decided to go too and be Methodists. Said he won't sure he wanted religion but any church that said nature created man free seemed a good place to be.

As Ned worked all day and as I needed to be back to serve the Colonel before evening, I never did get to see his home or meet Francie, but I did learn what the gentlemen thought about this Methodist church and neighborhood where Ned lived. I one day hear the Colonel in a lively conversation with a man named Dr. Benjamin Rush who lived in Philadelphia. Dr. Rush must have written something about how he thought they should get rid of slavery in Pennsylvania, and I hear him tell the Colonel that the free black folks were doing just fine down where Ned lived. The Colonel sees surprised to hear this and says something about the low vices of slaves, and Mr. Rush disagrees. He says slave children should be free and that whites should pay to send them to school. I listened for the Colonel to say something, but he don't say much more than when I asked him if he knew about that Quaker school for colored children.

Later, I thought about all this and couldn't help but wonder if I was included in that mention of slaves having low vices. A few days later I learn that Dr. Rush had wrote a whole book about freeing slaves and it stirred quite a pot among the delegates.

But I don't reckon the men at the Congress spent a whole lot of time talking about us slaves. They was pretty riled up over what had been happening up in Boston. It seems that after that fight in Concord, the militia chased the Redcoats back to Boston. Then they said maybe as many as 15,000 militia came out of all those towns up there and surrounded the city and kept the soldiers trapped. But that don't stop British ships from coming into the city and bringing more soldiers. Everyday riders kept coming into Philadelphia bringing word of all was happening up there.

So the Congress finally decides someone needs to go to Boston and be in charge of what they was calling the Continental Army. Now as I have said, the Colonel was a most respected man and each day I dressed him in his new military uniform, and with his height and bearing he certainly looks the part of a commander-in-chief, so I won't surprised to learn he was chosen. And I got to admit I was mighty proud they picked my Colonel, but he won't a colonel no more – he was now General Washington and that's what I have called him ever since.

Chapter 6

Well, by this time the General is mighty famous. As we left for Boston in mid June of '75 scores of folks come out to send us off. My master looks his usual splendid self in his blue uniform coat, and I looks pretty good too 'cause he tells me to wear my finest red coat – one he had made special for me – and also he gives me this bright red turban that I proudly wore and always feel gives me kind of a rank in the army – maybe even lets me pretend I'm something more than a slave. Anyway, many famous people was there for the sendoff. I remember Mr. John Adams who was said to be the man who come out most strongly for my master to be commander-in-chief. And two other military men was there too. They was later both generals themselves – but not as high ranking as my General. They were Charles Lee and Phillip Schuyler, and I got to know them both during the war.

We traveled north, first to New York where folks must a heard we was coming. Much to my surprise, the General has Giles stop the coach and has me fetch the fine white plume from his satchel. Then he fastens it to his hat and says it's to be part of his uniform from then on. He puts on his bright purple sash too and gets out of the coach and mounts Blueskin. Guess he thought riding a big white horse made a better show. We was surely not going to be unnoticed no more, and indeed a military band shortly shows up and marches along with us into the city.

As I recall we don't linger long in New York, 'cause the next day word come down from Boston sayin' a big battle had taken place up there. Seems the local militia from Massachusetts had control of a big hill called Breeds Hill, that overlooked the city, and the Redcoats wanted to chase them off. We learned the British did in fact take the hill, but they lost a lot more men than the militia, and as the folks in Boston grieved for their dead they also kinda felt they fought so good it was like a victory. Later we learned that this big battle was called the Battle of Bunker Hill, but I never knew why it was called that 'cause when we got there we learned Bunker Hill never saw no fighting.

When we get close to Boston, the militia, which I guess I should really be calling the Continental Army, had already heard the General was coming to be in charge. I won't sure how those Massachusetts boys was going to take to this, but when they see the General everybody starts to wave their hats and cheer. By this time it was July and very hot. The militia had already been pretty idle for a couple of weeks since that big battle on Breeds Hill, and I hear the General mutter they looked like a ragtag undisciplined bunch. I could see they was just a bunch of regular white folks – farmers, woodsmen, clerks, and they dressed in plain homemade cloth. But I had seen his concerns with the Alexandria militia, and I knew this was not the General's view of what an army should look like. What's more their tents was messy, clothes scattered about, campfires smoldering, men bathing naked right along the road for all to see, and worse – open latrines. It don't much look like no army – even to me. And the General blamed it on the officers – and let them know it right away. They don't seem to be in command of no one, mingling with the soldiers and even giving shaves and haircuts.

First thing the General did was set up headquarters in a place they called Cambridge which overlooks the city of Boston itself. He took over a pretty fine house almost as big as the mansion at Mount Vernon, and set it up so I even had my own small closet. Then he tried to get to know the men who would be his general officers. He don't know but one or two and a course they don't know him either, but from what I could tell they all accepted that he was the one in charge. And he started changing things right away – said officers should dress like officers – wear different colored plumes in their hats to show their rank, and then use that rank to get some discipline and get things cleaned up.

I knew things was bad my own self, 'cause as we rode through the camps there was this vile smell with open latrines all over the place – several close to a creek where men got drinking water. Even this poor slave knew places like that was just asking for sickness. The General said the officers had to make the men take pride in their army and to do that they had to first take pride in themselves – and that meant cleaning up. But taking pride was going to be hard because everywhere I saw tents that was tore, some shelters just with boards on three sides, some made of grass and sod, others of branches kind of woven together. I never seen slaves live so poorly.

I hear him tell the officers that if the men don't obey orders they was to be punished. He was big on discipline and order – don't surprise me none, 'cause that was the way he ran Mount Vernon. He also said men had to be kept busy and had them start right away digging fortifications – breastworks he calls them – and trenches dug for miles between us and the British who was just over the hills in Boston. The army don't really need to hunker down in the trenches, but occasionally the Redcoats would fire shells our way – probably more to let us know they thought they was still powerful. The General kind of liked the shelling – said it made the men think more serious about their business. Fortifications would make the British think we had a real army even if we only had a rag tail bunch of men. And putting up a good face was important 'cause we was worse off than the British knew. Half the soldiers was sick, some had no muskets, and those that did had little gunpowder. It surely was a real mess.

Each morning when I placed the General's sword belt around his waist and fastened his silver spurs to his boots, I knew he was just raring to lead his army and take on the British. If he could, I was sure he would a just charged right in with cannons and muskets blazing. While I don't know nothing about military matters, I did know my General and he was not a patient man. It would not have surprised me if he tried to catch the British unawares with an immediate attack. But with all the undisciplined troops, I guess he realized this would be stupid – and in truth I guess it was just me thinking foolish because not only did he not have much gunpowder he had no cannon at all. Besides, I overheard all the other generals talk about how unready their units was, so the decision was to drill the troops, train them to follow orders, and try to get some supplies from the Congress to equip the men. Worrying about how to get the Redcoats out of Boston would have to wait until the troops was ready.

As for me, I was always kept busy 'specially with carrying messages from the General to all the other officers and waiting for their replies. Everyone soon knew who I was, and as I rode up they'd call out, "Here comes Billy." Sometimes this kind of notice don't go over too good with the other servants, and they was a bit standoffish with me.

And, of course, added to my loneliness was being gone from Onetta and Isaac. The General wrote to Mistress Washington just about everyday, and soon her letters began arriving too. I knew it wasn't my place to ask the General to inquire about my little family so I was quite surprised after a few weeks when the General told me that Mistress Washington had said to tell Billy that Onetta and Isaac were doing fine and sent their love. I was most grateful for the news.

The General had the notion it would be a good idea to send spies into the city to see what the Redcoats was planning. It must not a been too hard to sneak around as some of the spies ventured in and out of the city each day, and told of a bad situation there. It seems the smallpox was beginning to spread among the British soldiers. The General was fearful his army might catch it too if the men came in contact with people trying to flee the city. He put up guards all around to keep folks away from his army, but I'm sorry to say it soon spread among our soldiers as well. The General had his own immunity to the disease as he caught a mild case when he was younger, and I myself never come down with it. But we spent a lot of time separating the soldiers who was sick from the rest to try to stop the spread of it as much as possible.

My own situation continued to prove uncomfortable mainly because most of the other servants was white. The only other black servant I knew was Giles. We was smack in the middle of scores of white servants, and while we worked around camp I had a hard time adjusting to working with all the whites. There was meals to prepare, wood to haul and chop, clothes to wash, latrines to dig, not to mention all of the time it took to feed, water, and care for the horses. And it won't just work outside. It seemed like every day the General had visitors come to tell him how to fight this war – sometimes carriages full of them – and most of them started calling him, "Your Excellency." I guess he liked this all right, but most I remember is that all them visitors gave us household servants plenty to do just to feed everyone. Good thing there was a bunch of us to do the work – more than you might think 'cause a lot of the officers had two servants. And you don't have to be no general to have your own servant – many colonels, majors and even captains brought along their own boys. I was kind of in charge 'cause I belonged to the General, but I was also black and except for the servants from the South, most of them was white, and some of them don't cotton too much to me.

One thing surprised me was that I found some black soldiers in the Massachusetts regiment – not valets or servants but real soldiers! I even heard one of them, a man named Peter Salem, had been kind of a hero in that battle on Breed's Hill. I never got to meet him, but I talked with a couple of other black soldiers and learned they and their families had long been free, and when the cry went out for what they called Minutemen, they just joined up to defend their town and countryside just like the whites did. This was a big surprise to me, because I heard the General say the militias in Virginia was formed years ago mainly to prevent and put down any slave rebellions. And up there in New England free black men was actually in militias and had been killed fighting a white man's war. Or at least that's the way I saw it at the time.

But the General don't see it that way. I don't know if he did anything about the few black men who was already serving in the Massachusetts unit, and I heard of a few more in the Connecticut and Rhode Island militias, too – but I heard him order that no more black men was to be accepted in the army now that it was his. He was okay if they wanted to have some slaves digging ditches or doing the other hard work, but no more black men was to be soldiers in his Continental Army!

About this time the General comes up with a plan for action – but it won't going to be there at Boston, but rather up north in some place called Québec, up in Canada. Talk was that there was a lot of French people up there who never liked the British, and he thought maybe some of our soldiers who won't really needed in Boston – especially if we won't going to attack – could go up to Québec and get those French people to join the rebellion. The General chose Colonel Benedict Arnold for this and he shortly left with about 1100 soldiers. I think this was some time in September when the weather won't too bad, but when those boys got up into Maine and tried to go by boat upriver they had more trouble than they could reckon with. Boats capsized, powder was wet, supplies was lost, feet was frozen, their maps was bad, and then came early winter snow. It was so bad about 500 of the men showed up back in Cambridge at the end of October. Well, we don't know what happened to the rest of them until after winter – and then we learned it was pretty bad for our side. A couple a hundred men was killed or starved to death, and they don't come close to getting that place to join any rebellion. I hear the General say the whole campaign was a disaster.

But he had other worries too, and so did I. Mistress Washington wrote him that the smallpox had reached Mount Vernon. Several families out at Dogue Run had fallen sick and two people had died. The General was beside himself with worry for Mistress and I heard him say she might be better off with him at Cambridge where he could look after her. I guess that's when she started making plans to join him. I began hoping maybe she'd need a seamstress and would bring Onetta with her, but this was mostly just dreaming.

I was kept pretty busy with errands to run and messages to carry. There was maybe ten thousand soldiers spread from Cambridge to Charlestown to Dorchester, and this meant many miles to travel. And there was always a few skirmishes here and there with our boys shooting at the Redcoats and them firing back, so I'd have to carry messages from the General to the officers that was in charge of troops all around that part of Massachusetts.

While I was running these errands there was one thing striking to me that won't even about the soldiers or the war. Many times I found myself in the countryside outside Cambridge where there was many small farms. At first I found it an unusual sight to see that white men did all the work on the farms. While I knew there was only a few people of my own color living up there, I had not connected this with the fact that the hard work required to farm the land must be done by whites. In Virginia the only white men working on farms seemed to be almost as bad off as the slaves. While they was free, their clothes was just as tattered, their houses sometimes looked like they might fall down, their fences was in disrepair, and their children ran around just as barefooted as black children playing around a slave cabin. And I knew the General never thought much of these poor whites. I could tell by the way he talked to them that he considered them simple folks who should do whatever the gentlemen of his class said they should do. But here in New England I saw white men farming who seemed well-off, even if the work they did was the same as the work of Virginia slaves. Their houses was small, but mighty fine to look at – gardens all around and barns too with sheep and cows, and their own pigs. This was my first time to consider that it don't take a plantation with a hundred slaves to have a successful farm.

While I was starting to think about stuff I'd never before even considered, there was still this problem with a bored army. There was a few sharpshooters pecking away if a British soldier got careless or too close, and most of the soldiers drilled every day. And while they got good at it while they was drilling, when they returned to camp there won't that much to do. I remember once during the first heavy snowfall when discipline got so bad the General got himself right in the thick of it. The New England boys and the Virginia boys never did much get along, and one day the northern boys began teasing the Virginians about their clothes which was the same what was worn for hunting deer and pheasants and stuff. Well they started out just throwing snowballs at each other, and it might have been fun except some of the boys got mad and began throwing punches instead of snow. Before you know it about fifty men was in an all-out fight. Well, me and the General was out surveying the troops when all this happened and he sees it, spurs Nelson right in the middle of it. He leaps from the saddle, throws the reins of his bridle into my hands and proceeds to the two tallest and brawniest savage looking riflemen and grabs each by the throat. He holds them at arms length and first shakes one and then the other. Everybody just stood there stunned at the rage and strength of the General. He next proceeds to shout orders to the officers who stood by while this happened. He understood that the troops was bored with all the standing around during the siege, but said that was no excuse for the breakdown in discipline, and he held the officers at fault.

Later on, it must have been sometime in November – I know it was after that big snowball fight – when I hear more talk about black men. It seems the same Governor Dunmore the General made pay for the gunpowder back in Williamsburg was now trying to get back at the Virginians who was rebelling against his King. Dunmore put out this order that any slaves owned by people who was against the King could just leave their masters and come over to the British side. If they agreed to join the British army or navy they would be set free. I heard it was called Dunmore's Emancipation

Proclamation and they even formed up a unit called the Ethiopian Corps. I wondered if my brother Frank and the other slaves at Mount Vernon had any way to hear about this.

Me and Onetta had talked time and again about what it would be like to be free. Mostly we liked our situations and knew we had it better than most any black folks we ever knew, so it was just something we talked about – never more than just talk. But now I won't sure about all the black folks who did hard labor twelve hours a day and had overseers who treated them not much better than cattle. Would they run away to join the British? Would it be better to have a British officer as your new master? Would treatment be any better just because they said you was free? And how long would this war last? Would you even live long enough to ever get to enjoy freedom? And what about your family and friends you would be leaving? Would you ever see them again? I was sure glad I don't have to worry about these things – even if at that time I sure missed my Onetta and Isaac.

Several times I heard the officers having arguments about black soldiers being in the army. General Greene had been in command of the siege around Boston until we arrived, and General Washington liked him just fine, and later on I guess he was sort of like a right-hand man, but when they talked about black soldiers, General Greene had a different take. He was a Quaker man, and they don't own no slaves, and like I said, there was already a few blacks in his Rhode Island regiment. So after we learned what Dunmore had done in Virginia, they had this council meeting with most all the high officers and voted on whether those New England free black men should be recruited for the army. Most of the officers agreed with General Greene that they should do it, but General Washington had not changed his mind. The answer was still, "No!" Said something like, "I don't want the Continental Army to be a refuge for runaway slaves." I don't know what that refuge meant but from the talking I learned it meant a kind of home for runaways. He said there was nothing he could do about preventing slaves in Virginia from joining up with Dunmore except write his friends and tell them to put out a heavy watch over their slaves, and he certainly won't going to do nothing to make that job worse.

Chapter 7

Long about December it started to get really cold and snowed quite a bit. I was glad to be warm in the Cambridge mansion, but a lot of the soldiers was cold and spent most days searching for firewood. I heard many just up and left for home – guess they thought it was too cold to fight anyhow. But in a way the General was glad for the snow. He had sent Colonel Knox up north to get as many cannon as he could and haul them back to Boston. There was this place called Fort Ticonderoga up in New York that Colonel Arnold and Colonel Ethan Allen captured from the British a few months earlier. The General said the cold and snow might make it easier for Colonel Knox to transport those cannon down to Boston by sled pulled by oxen. So about a hundred men left with high hopes that the rivers would be frozen and the snow would pack, but as for me I was just glad to be warm in that mansion at night.

The General was also in high spirits because Mistress Washington had written him some time ago she was fixing to leave Mount Vernon and join him there at Cambridge. Long about the middle of December he was expecting her any day and mentioned to me each morning he was worried about her traveling so far in bad weather. Most every day he was worried mightily. When she finally arrived it was with her whole family – Jacky, Jacky's wife Nellie, and a cousin – but I was looking at all of the black faces to see if my Onetta was one of the five household servants that was brought along. Sadly she was not, and I was surprised that no one even looked my way to offer a greeting – kind of cast their eyes away like they don't want to look at me.

That night after Mistress was mostly settled in her room in the mansion, she sent for me. She looked sad and I saw a tear in her eye. She said, "Billy, I have some very bad news for you – your little Isaac came down with smallpox just a few of weeks ago. Onetta was sick with worry so I called the doctor. But there was nothing he could do for the poor baby and he just got worse. Onetta nursed him best she could all week long, but the little boy died. We barely had him buried when Onetta fell sick with the smallpox too. I'm afraid she had no spirit left to fight the sickness, and again the doctor could do nothing for her. She died the very day we departed. I am so sorry to have to tell you this."

I couldn't believe what I heard. First I had been so hopeful that Onetta would be coming along, and now to hear that she had died – and little Isaac too. I don't know what to do. Mistress said Onetta was buried next to Isaac in the slave cemetery and she had a Christian service over them. Then she went on talking about the other black folks on the plantation who had also been sick and of another who died – but I hardly heard her.

Next morning the General don't say nothing to me about my loss. I knew he was busy, but I was certain Mistress told him, and I thought he might have mentioned something to me, but he don't. I tried to go about my work and was ready to leave with him for the morning troop inspection when he turned to me and quietly said maybe I should stay in the house today and he'd get one of the other boys to saddle up Nelson. That was just his way.

I don't remember much about the next few weeks. I thought about Frank and was worried he'd come down with smallpox too. How would I ever know? I cried at night thinking about those poor folks, but at dawn there was little time to dwell on my personal stuff as the mansion was busier than ever 'cause it was stuffed with all the new people from Mount Vernon plus all their servants added to the servants already there. On top of this all the officers seemed to think they should be in a nice warm house too. It was so crowded nobody could hardly turn around.

The General don't seem to notice. There was this new thing on his mind. Said he needed a special Life Guard unit. This was like his own personal little army – a bunch of soldiers who would follow along as we made our rounds inspecting the troops. He had always been fussy about dress – all the household servants at Mount Vernon had to be in clean livery everyday just in case there was visitors – which like I said was most every day. Well, even though the General don't seem to have much success getting funds for gunpowder and muskets from the Congress, he somehow was able to get special uniforms for his Life Guard. I guess he got what he wanted – everyone around him looking good – him up there sitting tall on Nelson – with his tail "nicked" so it would stand up high – me with my red coat and red turban – and about a dozen Guard dressed pretty much like the General and trailing behind.

Things picked up a bit by the end of January when Colonel Knox shows up with forty-two giant sleds loaded with about sixty cannon and mortars. He was quite the hero for managing to get them all the way from Ticonderoga to Cambridge especially considering how bad the weather had been. So now the General had his cannon and he was ready to drive the British out of Boston. "Not so fast," said the other generals. They had another one of these council meetings and reminded him that they was still short on gunpowder and seen British ships come into Boston Harbor with hundreds more soldiers. It seemed funny to me how the General listened to them about not going right away on the attack, but that he had not listened to them when they wanted to join up black soldiers. But I just listened – it sure won't my place to ask about this.

Well, what they decided was to try to trick the British. They made this plan for weeks and finally one night when it was 'specially dark they started shooting some cannon shells down on the city – not a lot, just enough to cover up what they was really doing which was wheeling a bunch of cannon over to a place called Dorchester Heights that was a lot closer to the city and close enough to the harbor where the British ships was docked so that if we did have ammunition we could hit them. At daylight the British woke up and saw all these guns looming over them, and I thought they would scared by it – and maybe they was, but I could see their officers rounding up the soldiers and scurrying around like they was getting ready to launch an attack to drive us off the heights. While the General is giving orders about which officer is to do what, all of a sudden the sky opens up and it starts to rain – and hard – then thunder and lightning, then wind and even harder rain. It went on like this for hours – half the night. The next day when it cleared up, the hill and the city was all muddy and much to my surprise we could see the Redcoat soldiers was not going to fight after all and was packing up to leave! They fired a bunch of cannon at us, but it was just to show off, 'cause their cannon-fire couldn't reach up the hills to Dorchester. The General was afraid the British would burn the city as they left, and there was some small fires, but none too big. There was still some shooting going on back and forth, but it don't amount to much. Mostly the British begin boarding their ships.

We watched all this for about ten days 'cause there was about nine thousand troops to load up and it took over a hundred ships to do it. What a sight! We sat on horseback each day watching the whole thing. And a big bunch of civilians went too – the General called them loyalists or Tories – and said he was glad to be rid of them. Later we went down into Boston and found destruction everywhere. Main thing the General was worried about was smallpox might still be everywhere, so most of the army stayed away. Some buildings was burned completely, even churches. Those still standing had broken windows; lots of porches was half tore off, and barns and stables was empty. The people was a sight too. There was some that came out to cheer as we rode by, but most just looked shocked – and I guess they worried about how the army would treat them. But I knew the General would be fair – he even threatened the troops if they mistreated the townsfolk, even if some of them was still for the King.

While everyone was excited about the Redcoats leaving Boston, the General got quite a bit of bad news. We knew from earlier that the expedition he sent north with Colonel Arnold to capture Quebec had gone very badly. But then reports came in that our soldiers who stayed up there through the winter had tried to put a siege on that city. It failed mightily. Some died from smallpox or frostbite and lay buried in the snow and ice, and then we heard that the main army was sitting ducks as their powder got wet and they was shot while trying to find safety. Before it was over about 400 of our boys had been killed or captured, and Colonel Arnold had a bad leg wound. What little army was left had no food or supplies and was sure to be captured. Almost as bad, the General learned the French people he thought would be against the British don't turn out that way. I heard him say over and over, "what a waste, what a waste."

The General decides his army must move south to New York, 'cause he's sure the British would next move on that city. But before we left there was one quite strange thing that happened at the Cambridge mansion. This young black woman shows up – and she's dressed like a lady. Much to my surprise I see soldiers from the Life Guard escort her up the steps, and then she comes in and sits down with the General! My place was to leave the room so I don't hear what was said, but later I did hear one of the officers say that the General received her with "a very courteous reception," and that Mistress Washington shook her hand and greeted her as well. My, oh my, what a strange thing. So I couldn't help myself. That night when I assisted the General with his undressing, I said, "I don't want to step out of place but I sure am curious about that fine dressed Negro woman who was here today." The General looks at me kind of funny like he is thinking about whether he should talk about this or not and then he says, "Billy, do you know what a poet is?" Well no, I'd never even before heard the word, but then as nice as can be he tells me that this young black woman is a poet – a person who writes stories kind of like a song, and that she had written one about the General. He goes on to say the poem she wrote had been in several newspapers and told of what a fine man and great leader the General was. I think I said out loud, "My, oh my!" So he proceeds to tell me her name is Phyllis Wheatley. She's only twenty-two years old and he says she has written a bunch of poems that educated white folks think is really good. And then he says to me, "I'm just amazed that a slave can achieve this kind of talent."

Well, of course I don't know what to make of this. By this time I'd been the General's valet for about four years and I'd heard him speak to black folks most often, and I'd never heard anything pass his lips toward a slave other than a command or wanting to know why something won't done just so, or some dressing-down or other. While he was not severe with me, I had certainly learned it was not my place to be casual with him, and I was certain he considered the colored race beneath him. And now he can have a "courteous reception" with a slave girl – but he can't even mention my Onetta and Isaac to me when they died.

Chapter 8

Well, I tried to put these things out of my mind and the nice spring weather helped. Everything was just starting to blossom when we starts south for New York. The General left most of the Massachusetts boys in Boston just in case the Redcoats come back. The trip was about 200 miles but it seemed longer, 'cause every town and hamlet we passes through wants to have a big celebration for "His Excellency" – which was what more and more people was calling him. Usually he would ride in the coach with Mistress until the outskirts of town and then mount Blueskin to ride with what he said was more dignity, and it was true the people could see him better on a tall white horse. His Life Guard followed smartly close behind and I sits as tall as I can in the saddle to help out with this dignity business.

When we get to New York City– really just the tip of the island of Manhattan – the General leaves the army there under the command of General Charles Lee. He seemed like kind of a strange man to be a general – never dressed good and always had about six or more hound dogs yipping and following him around. Anyway, the two generals made plans to build two forts to protect the city – one on each side of the Hudson River, and decides to name them after themselves. After giving General Lee orders and such for construction of the forts we take Mistress on to Philadelphia – again with the Life Guard as our escort.

The General has two reasons for wanting to go to Philadelphia. First, he has bottled up his anger about that Congress for a long time, and wants to go there to talk to those men – 'cause he couldn't see where they had been any help at all to him with that siege at Boston. It won't just not receiving supplies; he was most angry cause the men had been lied to about their pay. Fact was, they hadn't received none at all, so how could the General blame them for leaving to go home when enlistments was up? How could he get men to join up if there was to be only lies and no pay?

But while he's pleading his case with the Congress, everybody gets all excited because they get word that the British hired a bunch of soldiers they called Hessians to come over and fight for them and that there might be as many as two hundred ships carrying them and other Redcoat soldiers – and also a mess of British war ships. The General tells the Congress if the British was sailing for New York it would be hard to defend the place as it was completely surrounded by bays and rivers – just right for the British navy. But the Congress says New York must be held, and a course the General says he'll do it – and I guess he just hoped they would keep their word about supplies and pay for the men.

The second reason we was in Philadelphia was that the General wants Mistress to take the smallpox prevention. This was something called inoculation where they actually give a person some of the disease – and it was suppose to make you sick but not kill you – and then you couldn't get smallpox no more. It don't sound like a great idea to me and I was glad the General don't want me to do it, but Mistress stayed in Philadelphia to recover from the treatment while we went back to New York.

I thought the most interesting thing 'bout New York was you never knew who was on your side. Lots of folks was still loyal to England 'cause of all the trade they did, and having a war was ruining their business. The General said many folks had just been so used to being British citizens that they felt loyal to the King, and saw the troubles in Massachusetts and Virginia as none of their business. He was supposing there might even be more loyalists in New York than patriots. But the General wanted everyone to be treated fairly, so unless those people actually did something against the army, he wants his soldiers to leave them alone. But this was sometimes hard because the soldiers mingled with the citizens everyday – bought stuff from them – drank ale with them in taverns – and got involved with the women.

One thing surprised me was how many black folks was in the city. I thought we was still up North, but it turns out New York had a big slave trade for many years and colored was found everywhere – on farms, working in shops, driving wagons, and a course as household servants. It seemed really more like I was in the South. I was told there was a lot of free blacks in the city too, but I don't have no free time like in Philadelphia when I went and talked to Ned, so I don't get to know any.

There was a lot of fear in the city, too. First the General comes in with his army – about nine thousand men – and like I said, discipline was not always the best. And then they hear British ships was coming with thousands more soldiers. I couldn't blame the people for wondering what would happen to their city. Fighting for certain was to be coming – and they surely heard what bad shape Boston was in – and that was just with small battles. So I won't surprised to see many folks just pack up their furniture and children and set off in wagons – hundreds of them.

It was no secret there was bound to be a big battle sometime soon, but in the meantime the General has to find some place for a headquarters, and just like up in Cambridge, he finds this big house in Manhattan called Richmond Hill. It's big enough for the general officers and all us house servants, and becomes 'specially important to me as it's where I get to know Margaret Thomas. She was one of the servants who came down from Massachusetts but I barely knew her then. But she knew about me, and knew about my grieving over Onetta and Isaac.

Then long about July, we hear those folks in Congress has come up with this big declaration. Said the colonies was an independent country – no more a part of England. Well this don't come as no surprise to me – I'd been on the road with the General for over a year and we'd been fighting Redcoats the whole time. I wondered why it took so long for that Congress to look around and see what's been going on. So the General has all his officers assemble the troops in the hot sun and read this entire declaration to them. The troops all cheered, so I guessed the Congress finally done something right. But there was stuff I heard that puzzles me. Words in that declaration kept saying the King had been treating them like slaves. Well, I don't know any white men who was slaves or even treated like slaves. What did this independence business have to do with slaves – except that some of the first words I hear said that all men was created equal. So was this war about making black men equal and free too?

Well, over the next few days I keep trying to figure out how I can ask the General about all this, but we was always so busy running around checking on fortifications and sick soldiers there was no time to approach the subject. And then toward the middle of the month no words in any document seemed to matter very much, 'cause when we looked out into the harbor all we see is a sea of tall masts! As one officer said, "it looked like all London was afloat and in our backyard." They said altogether there was about four hundred ships, and they guessed over 30,000 troops – and all there to drive us out of New York.

And that's exactly what General Greene said we should do. He says there is no way 9,000 troops can defend the city against so many – and besides many of the ships was gunboats and could just fire away at us. The General thought the cannon he had brought down from Boston and placed in Forts Lee and Washington on both sides of the Hudson River would protect Manhattan from the British gunboats. But pretty soon the British ships come sailing down the river and none of them cannon in those forts can hit even one of them. The General says, "Why should I hold these forts if they are useless to strike the enemy?" But he must have just been thinking out loud 'cause then he orders General Greene and General Lee to each hold one of the forts.

I thought General Greene was right about leaving Manhattan, and we should skedaddle, but the General says, no – he had a plan. I never thought he was too keen on this plan, but kind of felt like his honor was at stake, and he couldn't just up and run.

A few days go by and the British don't do much except tease us by running their ships up and down the river where our cannon still can't reach them. Long about August, the Redcoat generals send a boat over with a bunch of high officers who say they want peace not war. All the General has to do was say we would be loyal to the King and send our troops home. Going home sounds pretty good to me, but I know it's too late for this, and the General thanks them for the attempt to avoid more bloodshed, but he knew that with all those ships and armies bearing down on us, to accept their terms would really be to surrender. So when they left he right away starts sending his troops in different places he thinks best for defense of the city. The General told the troops they was fighting for their country and for freedom. He says they was going to make history by creating a new nation. But he also says he won't broke with no cowards, and he would fight his own self as long as he still had a leg or arm. This seemed to inspire the men – but I knew the truth was we was greatly outnumbered, and when the fighting began it was going to be awful bad.

First off, the General sends about a third of the army over to Brooklyn, where he thinks they might surprise the British. But they scarcely gets there when a barrage of cannon fire rains down on Manhattan. It goes on for what seems like hours and liked to scare to death the womenfolk who had stayed in the city, and they come running out of their homes screaming and trying to find some place to hide. And worse our boys in Brooklyn don't surprise nobody. They fought well but the Hessian and British soldiers overwhelmed them. I heard Hessian soldiers bayoneted men to death even after they surrendered and I heard some of the men took prisoner were harnessed like horses and made to pull the British cannon.

The fighting went on for days. We'd be in Manhattan one day and across the river in Brooklyn the next. I don't think I ever slept as we dashed from one unit to another. The Redcoats had their own pretty good sharpshooters and I heard several musket balls whiz by my ear, though surely intended for the General. After days of fighting and retreating and fighting some more, the troops was greatly outnumbered at every battle. The General knew we better take what men we can and sneak back across the East River to Manhattan. I spends three days up and down the shore for miles looking for boats for the men – I guess we stole quite a few, and we was able to get maybe a hundred little rowboats to carry several thousand troops back across the river. On the foggiest of nights the General tells a small party of men to keep the campfires burning brightly to fool the British, and then for the main army to come quietly down to the river. Some of them boats made as many as seven trips back and forth that night to ferry all the men. Oars were bound with rags to muffle the sound. The General insists on being in the last boat to leave shore, but I was really last 'cause I helped push the boat off. Later it was said the evacuation from Brooklyn was an "amazing feat" – but we all knew better. The General should never had made this battle, and I heard him say we was lucky the British generals had not moved more quickly or they could have cut us down before we got across the river.

We was a pretty desperate army by the time we marched down the streets of Manhattan. Many men was sick, all in wet clothes, and all confused. Worse, there was not enough food or shelter for the men. Some began looting houses – and not just for victuals – but just out and out stealing stuff. The General was so mad at this he had the officers search the knapsacks of the troops and threatened to shoot the thieves. Even worse still, the people was now so angry at our army that any patriotism they felt before the shooting was now fading fast.

General Greene said things was so bad we should burn what's left of Manhattan and get off the island. He said there was so many Tories he suspected most people would welcome the British when they came across the river. While the generals argue over whether burning was the right thing to do, the Redcoats land boat after boat of troops in several places on the island. Soon there was battles all over the place and we was on the losing side in all of them. There was really nothing to do but move off the island – and fast. But the General was still trying to rally his troops. We went riding up and down alongside the retreating soldiers trying to make them stop and make a stand. The General makes a fine target waving his sword in the air directing troops, and I think he's bound to get killed. Me, I'm riding as low as I can and keep looking back to see who was behind. Once when I turn in my saddle I see a Hessian soldier aim his musket right at my head. I close my eyes and spur Chinkling to the left and hear a musket ball go whizzing right by my ear. Wonder was it don't hit me or Chinkling. Bullets was flying as we raced across to Harlem Heights where there was some hills that give us some safety. The General finally locates his Virginia riflemen – rangers he calls them – and those boys is fine shots. They make a stand that's finally able to stop the British troops chasing us.

But we don't stay there long 'cause the British always has more men they can land on shore. That next morning when I hand the General his telescope and he surveys the waterfront below, he sees about four thousand soldiers where there was none the night before. So we skedaddle again – this time to a place called White Plains on the other side of the Bronx River. It was high ground so the General orders the officers to have their troops throw up breastworks and defend the place.

Meanwhile the British decide they don't cotton much to those forts, Lee and Washington, even if they was no threat to British ships. So when the General gets word that Redcoats are headed toward Fort Washington, he decides we're going to ride down there and see what's what. We meet up with General Greene and General Putnam at Fort Lee and row over to the other side. We was about a mile above the fort when I seen more solders in one spot than I'd ever seen before. The General says there must be about thirteen thousand British and Hessian soldiers surrounding the fort where we only had about three thousand men trying to defend it. The cannon in the fort did pretty good at first and cut down about a hundred enemy soldiers in the first wave that rushed forward. But soon we could see that the fort would be overrun. As it turned out the fort became a death trap for our soldiers. We could see it all, and the General had tears in his eyes as he saw all the killing, and those of our army who was not bayoneted to death was captured. Later we learned the prisoners was placed on prison ships in the Hudson River, where most either starved to death or died from sickness.

And a few days later it won't no better with that Fort Lee either. But this time the General realizes it's useless to try to defend the fort and ordered its evacuation. We saved about two thousand of our men and more than a hundred cannon and supplies and pulled them all back to New Jersey with the rest of the army. It was a wonder the British generals don't see fit to chase after us 'cause we was a sorry lot. The men was ragged, many without shoes on their feet; some wrapped in blankets, many wounded. But worse, they looks like their spirits was broken – and some of the officers too. As we marched across New Jersey, I see men too tired and defeated to stick with the army – and they starts leaving – maybe more than a hundred a day. And I can't blame them. Poor souls, I thought; the only way they'd make it to their homes was by pillaging off the land – and the truth was many who stayed with the army also resorted to this. By the time we reached New Brunswick we'd lost maybe two thousand men and we was left with an army of less than four thousand.

The General said many times he hoped more men might be recruited for the army. But this was surely not to be the case in New Jersey where the British army was making most everybody sign loyalty oaths to the King of England. As our army marched mostly barefoot through the cold of

December, I was mighty glad to be astride Chinkling. Funny how being a slave in my situation gave me many comforts beyond the common soldier. I don't have long to ponder what at the time seemed like good fortune, 'cause we don't stay in New Brunswick very long. The General thought we should head toward Philadelphia to try to defend it in case the British won't satisfied to stay in New York for the winter.

As it turned out, the main part of the British army did stay in New York, with just a smaller part in New Jersey. So that gives the General a new plan. As wore out as the troops was, he has them march south on the Pennsylvania side of the Delaware River and by the middle of December we make camp across the river from a town called Trenton.

In those times it was hard for any army to keep secrets 'cause you never know if the folks living on the land was patriots or Tories. As it turned out we get good information from patriots that an army of Hessians is guarding Trenton, but even if them Hessians get word where we are, they probably think the bad weather will prevent any attack. But my General thinks the weather is just right for his big plan to cross over the river and surprise them. Once again we need boats and I go up and down the river for miles searching for them. This time we need big ones for the horses and cannon, and I find some barges used for hauling iron ore. Problem was when he decides to cross it's Christmas Day and colder than ever. There was ice everywhere, and in truth only about a third of our army make it across. I won't in the boat with the General, 'cause he wants me in one of the barges caring for the horses. The rocking boat and sounds made by the ice cracking underneath nearly scare Nelson and Chinkling half to death – and me too – but we finally make it across. When we get to the other side we mount up and the soldiers march real quiet over the snow into Trenton and surprised the bejesus out of them Hessians.

Later, folks said this was the finest victory the General ever had as we lost only a handful of men and the Hessians lost over 900 – either killed, wounded, or captured. The men was excited by the victory – a bunch of them found some rum and did a bit of celebrating – but most just wanted to go home 'cause their enlistments was up in just a few days – the end of the year. The General makes another plea to the worn out soldiers to try to get them riled up again, and I was amazed at how the men listened to him. It was like courage and determination just kind of washed over their faces as he spoke. Most all of them agreed to stay, and it won't long before we was back in the thick of battle.

The British had this general by the name of Cornwallis who was pretty angry about losing Trenton and he sent an even bigger force against us. The General makes this slick move making like he's going to stand and fight, but during the night, just like when we escaped across the river up in Brooklyn, he quietly sends the main part of his army around the left flank of the British and we march twelve miles to the town of Princeton. The next morning we surprised the British in that town so bad I later overheard a Redcoat prisoner say he thought we had come down out of the clouds.

It was a big surprise all right, but not so easy as Trenton. The British fought hard – so hard that at one point our men started to panic. This was one of those times I thought the General would surely die. He tells me to wait five minutes before coming forward with another horse and then he spurs Nelson out between the two armies yelling and waving his sword for his men to stand and fight. When he gets them reorganized, he leads the charge up this long hill. I figure Nelson might go down at any moment so I come rushing up from the rear just in case. Well, I guess you heard what happened – the British soldiers must a thought they was being attacked by a crazy man, 'cause they stopped firing and shortly turned tail, and before I knew it they was in full retreat with our boys chasing after them. It reminded me of a foxhunt like we used to have here at Mount Vernon.

By now I was used to following the General into danger, but that Princeton battle was the worst yet. The General sometimes don't really know how to do the generaling. I been privy to enough planning sessions to know that generals is supposed to make the plans and then lay back and watch the lower officers make the battle. But not my General – no sir, he has to ride right in the thick of it and lead every charge. He gets his victory at Princeton just fine, and again loses only a few men – but I swear a hundred bullets was fired at him as he spurred Nelson into the thick of battle. Sometimes I could hardly keep up with him 'cause he would turn and whirl over here and then over there. One general said it was like there was an unseen shield around him protecting him – and if this was true I was sure glad, 'cause it protects me too.

Chapter 9

We spent the rest of that winter at Morristown, New Jersey, and while there was some skirmishes in the countryside, me and the General mostly stayed out of it. He was glad to be in a place where mail could again find him, and was able to hear from his man Lund and from Mistress Washington. The General was always wanting to tell Lund what he should be doing, and always wanted to hear what was going on. So he finally gets letters and hears all the news about his family's health, about who just been elected to serve in the Continental Congress, about the new construction on the mansion, about how the livestock was faring, and which of the gentlemen's wives had just born a baby. He learns about fencing that needs replacing, how many gallons of whiskey was made at the distillery, and just about anything else they thinks the General might want to know. But nobody thought it proper to tell this old slave anything about the only family I had left. Nobody ever sent no word about my brother, Frank. I had long been accustomed to living just for the aid and pleasure of the General, but I couldn't help but think he might care enough about me to inquire about my only kin.

One day while powdering his hair I asks him if he had word about any more deaths at Mount Vernon from the smallpox. He advised, yes several slaves had died over the last months. "Anybody I know?" I asks. He tells me their names, but I don't know them and so I am somewhat relieved. But then he starts talking about being mighty worried about smallpox there at our camp, and how he's trying to get a doctor from down in Philadelphia to come up and start inoculating the soldiers. I again found it hard to ask him anything personal – still felt it was not my place.

We was quartered in an old tavern not nearly as large as that nice mansion in New York – that I suppose was now enjoyed by the British generals. It was funny but even after the General's victories at Trenton and Princeton the Congress was still slow to provide funds and support for the army. Our provisions was so bad the General had to make sure our soldiers don't go raiding out in the countryside to steal from the people. The General wants folks to look up to the patriot army, 'specially after it had shown it could fight and win some battles.

Another problem was lots of folks swore a loyalty oath to the British – I guess they had to – but now the General gives them a chance to take it back. Some folks couldn't take their swear back, but he said not to harm them. He just makes them leave their homes and go over to the British. There was no real battle lines that winter. Sometimes our scouting parties bumped into those of the British, and small battles was fought – but they was really fighting just to get provisions. I learned then that hungry troops is just like hungry slaves – everybody does what they has to – we all has to eat.

One day this man named Robert Morris shows up at the tavern. I'd not seen him before and noted he traveled without any servant. He has this brown satchel he carried like it was kind of heavy, and goes into this private talk with just the General. Well, of course, I don't know what they was talking about, but a few days later the General tells me he wants me to carry a message. This wasn't unusual as I carried messages up and down the line most every day. But this time he tells me to take off my red turban and red coat, and slip on a deerskin jacket. I wonder to myself – what in the world? Then he hands me a letter and tells me where to deliver it. I notice it's a lot heavier than just paper, but he don't tell me what's in it and a course I don't ask. Well, I can see it's got some writing on it, but at this time I still can't read so I just deliver it where he tells me – to a man in town at a print shop and I should ask for Mr. Culper. I do what I am told, deliver the letter, and don't think too much about it until the next week when I'm given the same kind of letter to carry.

This one is even heavier than the first one, and after I'm mounted and away I'm curious and shakes the letter.

There's stuff movin' around inside and it don't take long for me to guess it's coins - and from the weight I'm guessing gold coins. Well, just about every week I'm shed of my red turban and coat and I'm off delivering a letter like this to Mr. Culper. Sometimes I meet him at the print shop, other times at a gatehouse by a bridge, and another time at somebody's home. So I'm wondering - where did the money come from? The General's always complaining he don't have money enough to pay the troops yet he's sending me off to pay someone I'd never seen before and who don't give me nothing in return. I keep thinking, what's this money for? And why do I never hear the General talking to nobody about it?

Well, it wasn't unusual to see the General spending lots of time at his writing desk. Seems there was always folks he needs to write to, so I'm used to seeing him tied up with letters and such. But one day I see him writing in a strange little book. It's got lines going up and down and across - don't look like any letters or orders I'd ever seen. So I'm kind of peeking over his shoulder, and he sees me. I thought he might be mad, but he says, "Does this look like strange writing?" I said I was sorry to be poking my nose where it don't belong, but he says to me, "No, since I've got you taking all the risk, maybe it's time you know what's going on."

He asks me if I know the letters I'd been carrying had money inside, and I said yes, I suppose I did, and I'd wondered about it all. He told me he don't want any of his officers to be carrying these letters. Says if they was out of uniform and the British caught them they could be hanged as spies. He says he's using the money to pay for information, and that nobody thinks much of colored boys running errands here and there and he figures I'll be okay. Then he says he knows it's dangerous but he trusts me to do whatever he asks.

Well, I hardly knows what to say. It's the first time he's talked to me like this - kind of like I'm important and worth an explanation. I just kind of stammer and thank him mightily for trusting me so with important stuff and I'd always do whatever he wants me to. He says these letters I've been carrying and the money are very important and the only people who know anything about them are in this little book he's been writing with all the funny lines and it's called a code, and it has to stay a secret. I nods my head and tells him I won't say nothing about nothing to nobody, and he kind of smiles and says he knows he can trust me.

Well, this kinda changed everything between me and the General. I don't mean it changed what I did – I kept running errands, riding with him on troop inspections, shining his boots, stropping his razor, laying out his clothes, powdering his hair and all. But the change was how I felt about him. He was still my master, for sure, and the biggest General, of course, but now we was also two men who shared a trust that nobody else knew about – and I began hoping that maybe one day I could talk to the General about this whole slavery business.

Chapter 10

While the army was cooped up in Morristown all winter, the General tried mightily to get his troops healthy. There was always a good number of men quarantined and recovering from the smallpox inoculations. But sanitation was always what he stressed most – clean clothes and well-kept latrines especially. And he also tried to get the soldiers to eat better – more vegetables and salads especially. A course, he was always trying to get them to cut back on their drinking even though they got a daily ration of rum. He said they should water it down and spread it through the day instead of gulping it down in one swig to try to get a little drunk. And a course when the men foraged through the countryside they was always looking for alcohol of any kind, and the General tried to stop this. But the General was also looking out for other spirits too – what he called the spirit of the mind. He encouraged music of all kinds, and singing too, but he don't like beating them drums too loud at all hours. Church, too, he said was good for the men; had them elect chaplains to conduct services and was always talking to them about Providence being on their side 'cause they was fighting for something noble. He tells the other officers to make sure everyone remembered the cause – a new country with all men equal – but I knew he really don't mean all men.

That March the General come down sick. I did what I could – put cold cloths on his forehead to take down the fever, made him drink this stuff the doctor said was good for him, and stayed with him through the night. He don't really get much better until Mistress comes up from Philadelphia and that perks up his spirits and his body.

She'd only been there a little while when one day Mistress decides what all the officers needs is the company and polite society of women. She arranges dinners and invites gentle women in the town to attend. They did dances and when the weather permitted even had these social horseback jaunts through the countryside. Well, a course, all us servants was busy making sure all these folks had a good time, but I confess I wasn't so interested in all the socializing they was doing 'cause I had the company of a young woman of my own.

As I said before, Margaret Thomas was one of the General's household servants ever since New York. She was a free black woman and a good cook, and as we'd known each other now for almost a year we had seen quite a bit of each other. At first she listened to me talk about Onetta and Isaac, and her sympathetic ear was I guess what attracted me to her. Before long though we became involved and pretty soon decided we would be married. Well, there was no broom jumping or pig roast with family and friends – we just told people we was married and so we was. I'll always remember those months at Morristown as we was both very happy and together whenever possible.

It was round 'bout that time I met two men the General really liked and became important to him. One was Alexander Hamilton, a young artillery officer, and the other was from France, and only nineteen, by the name of the Marquis de Lafayette. It was a fancy name, but he really took to the General and sort of looked up to him almost like a father. I always thought maybe the General took a special liking to Lafayette because he not only came to help with fighting the British, but brought a boatload of food and munitions with him too. Colonel Hamilton was the most energetic man I ever seen, and after a couple months the General can hardly do without him. He's helping with the General's letter writing, giving his own advice about the troops, riding around seeing generals – even telling them what to do. As far as I can see the General is happy with everything he does. Folks say Hamilton don't like slavery, but I never talk to him about it, and he certainly don't mind giving me an order or two. Like him or not, he was always helping with decisions, and it turned out he served the General all through the war and even later when the General became President.

Another thing happened during that winter and spring at Morristown, and I was very happy to see it. The General finally changed his mind about having black soldiers. He don't change about freeing any slaves if they fought – said that was up to the states, but if any colored man was already free and wanted to join his army he said it was now all right. Mostly it was up to each regimental commander what the black solders actually did, but from my eyes there was plenty who carried muskets and joined the battles. I told the General one morning that I was right glad there would be black soldiers 'cause they would fight hard to prove they was just as good as the whites. I said that's how it always is when you know you are looked down on – you have to work harder. He don't say nothing, but I got the sense he understood what I meant.

By summer those spies the General has been paying gives him some grim news. British General Howe who chased us out of New York was getting ready to try to take Philadelphia. We learn from spies that over two hundred ships was headed up the Chesapeake Bay loaded with soldiers. Well, the General gets all the troops hustled up and we get to Philadelphia first. The General wants to make a show that his troops was ready to defend the city, so he has this big parade and for two hours our army with twelve men abreast marched smartly through the city. They all had this green sprig in their hats the General said stood for victory, and they was dressed in the best they had, which for many men won't too much. But I thought they looked pretty good marching to the beat of fife and drums, and with the Life Guard Unit we looked good too on horseback leading the whole parade all through the city. People cheered and waved their hats, so I guess the General got what he wanted – the support of the city he was about to defend.

But having a parade was easier than keeping the British out of Philadelphia. The General decides his army will stop the British at a place called Brandywine Creek. He has his generals place the troops, and it seems to me he's laid a pretty good trap for them British. But we don't know that

General Howe has spies too and already figured out the General's plans and splits his army into several parts and comes at our army from different directions. In soldier talk they says he has outflanked us. The General was hard pressed to figure out what to do. He don't lead no charges like he usually does. We watched from a hilltop and see a bunch of little battles, but the gist of it was that the General has to retreat to save the army.

They learn about this battle in Philadelphia and before you know it there was wagonloads of people coming our way fleeing the city before the British march in. The Congress was leaving too, and some of them rode up to the General and was angry that he don't defend the city better. But he tells them that we're not licked yet and he makes another plan to attack the British before they actually get to the city.

General Howe rested his army at a place called Germantown, and the General makes his plan to attack there. But before he attacks, I get sent on an errand that changes my whole way of thinking about this war. I'm sent off to warn General Wayne that spies tell us part of the British army is marching his way, and he should cut off north and join the rest of the army at Germantown. He's supposed to be at a place called Paoli's Tavern, and I take off on Chinkling. It was a couple hours' ride and I can hear gunfire from a long way off. When I finally get to the tavern it's still – nobody around – just the smoke from battle. At first I don't see no one, but as I ride on I see a body in the road – dead – and then another and another. Then I see what I will never forget – dozens of bodies – all blood stained corpses – must have been cut down by British bayonets and then it looked like they was cut further to pieces while they must have laid wounded. Their blue and brown clothes was all coated with the red of their blood – and swollen eyes popping out their heads. It was a pitiful sight. There was even these little streams of blood still flowing from their bodies and pooling along the road. I turn Chinkling around 'cause I don't want to see no more.

I must have been riding about a half hour and I see a sight almost as bad as the bloody bodies. This man comes staggering out of a house – I know he's one of ours cause I can see this green sprig still in his cap. Then a woman comes out screaming after him about stealing the only food she has for her children. He turns back and takes the butt of his musket and strikes her in the head and knocks her down. She falls hard, crying and he starts to kick her, but then he sees me. I'll never forget the look on his face. It was wild with rage and hate. He starts after me and I whirl Chinkling and ride away – not so much afraid for my own life but just so sad to see such a sight and know I can't do nothing about it.

As I rode back toward our camp near Germantown I kept seeing visions of all those bloody bodies and hearing the screams of that woman. I says to myself – this is what war is – just killing and hate. I seen killing before – and surely just by chance had missed being killed myself, but I never seen it like this. I wonder, is this what war does to men? Is this independence business worth all this hate and killing?

When I reached camp I run in and starts telling the General the British got to General Wayne before I did and I tell him about the massacre. He's pretty upset about it, but don't have time to do nothing 'cause just while I'm still talking Colonel Knox comes in the tent excited about this big stone house where he says British soldiers is holed up. Seems while I was away the General started the attack against General Howe's army, and Colonel Knox was leading the charge. Knox says, "There's a whole regiment in this house firing away at our soldiers and blocking the way to the main battle." The General asks why Knox can't just take his army around the house and leave it be. Colonel Knox says our army can't just leave the British in this house 'cause then they will be at the rear of our army when we go forward to attack. The officers hear this and start talking all at once giving their opinions until the General decides Colonel Knox is right. We ride out and the General orders Knox's regiment to storm the house. Turns out more than a hundred of our men was wasted trying to take that house, and as bad as that was, all the time spent doing it gives Howe time to set up against the General's attack.

But this time the General's not going to let this Germantown battle be like the one at Brandywine Creek. He's not just going to watch the battle. He sits up tall on Nelson and leads the charge himself. When he's got one regiment moving forward he pulls out and moves to another and leads the charge over there. I don't have no time to think about whether this war is right or wrong – I just follow along leading another horse in case Nelson goes down. It looks like our troops is doing pretty good, but then it starts to drizzle and this heavy fog rolls in and you can't see who you're shooting at. The upshot is we don't stop the British from moving on to Philadelphia, but the Continental Army fought pretty good, and those men in Congress must have thought killing a lot of British soldiers was a good thing, 'cause Congress gives the General a medal for his bravery.

Chapter 11

Well, I guess you'd probably like to know about Valley Forge – seems like most folks I talk to is interested in hearing about that winter. Indeed, that's where we went after those battles at Brandywine and Germantown. But that's jumping a little ahead 'cause something big happened before we went to winter quarters.

The General was still smarting over losing Philadelphia. He always liked honors and the medals he got, but he knew the truth was he was beat and driven out of the two biggest cities – New York and now Philadelphia. Since the Congress had to skedaddle too, he don't want to pull the army too far away in case the British try to capture those men. The Congress went to York, Pennsylvania to try to have their government there. So the General decides we should camp about twenty miles outside Philadelphia about halfway between York and Philadelphia. That's when he chose that place called Valley Forge.

He figures we would most probably have to spend the winter there and while we're riding around trying to see where to make headquarters and where the soldiers will live, he gets this big news. It seems that there's this place up north called Saratoga in New York state. I'd never heard of it, but I'd heard part of the Continental army was up there trying to stop another part of the British army that was coming down the Hudson Valley from Canada. The General had sent General Gates and General Arnold up there some months before with part of the army. Well, much to everyone's surprise we get word there was a battle at this Saratoga place and General Gates had this big victory. Not only did he win the battle but also his army captured a couple thousand British and Hessian soldiers. A course, we was all glad to hear this, but I could tell the General was a mite uneasy over all the fuss everyone was making about General Gates. I wondered if it could be 'cause the General only won little battles and General Gates had won a big one.

Well, Saratoga was a long way off and it don't change nothing for me, but one thing puzzled me was I heard the General talking about what to do with all them prisoners they captured. Turns out they ended up walking them prisoners all the way to Virginia and made them build their own prison barracks when they got there. I never could figure why they don't just build those barracks where they was instead of marching 600 miles from New England to Virginia.

Meanwhile we're still deciding on where to house the army and it starts to snow. Many men in the army has been marching and fighting all year in the same tore clothes, same shoes and same boots – and they was mighty wore out by the time winter set in. The General chooses this place at Valley Forge cause it's nice level clear land, but with plenty of woods close by to cut lumber and firewood. We had about four thousand soldiers he was trying to keep together, and he sets every one of them to work building huts for themselves. I never seen white men work so hard. They got in these teams of about twelve each and started cutting trees and splitting lumber. They hauled straw and mud for chinking and set to figuring out ways to put a roof on the cabins so they won't leak. The General even set a hundred dollar reward from his own pocket to the team that made the best roof. The others learned from this, and before very long there was over a thousand of these little cabins all set out like a little city with streets and everything. A course the cabins won't much for comfort – pretty small with ceilings so low a tall man could hardly stand up straight. There was just dirt floors and no windows 'cause there was no way to keep the weather outside, and doors was figured every which way. They reminded me pretty much of the slave cabins back at Mount Vernon.

I saw a change in the General during this time. He was upset by the condition of the men. Up to this time he would always complain that they looked so bad – not like an army should. But now he seemed to feel sorry for them. Many times he saw their bloody footprints in the snow, and clothes so ragged they was wrapped in blankets as they tried to do their work. Their hands was wrapped in rags, but the men kept at their work, and the General told them he was proud of them and liked what they done. He don't try to find no mansion like always before to set up for his headquarters – in fact we slept in a tent right beside the men until the cabins was mostly finished, and then he rented a small house from a man named Potts. But it was pretty pinched for room – his aides had to sleep downstairs on the floor, kind of in rows. Me and Margaret was lucky to sleep in the kitchen where she cooked. It was the warmest room in the house.

But it was conditions outside the house that was really bad. It was either so cold that the wind went right through you or when there was a bit of sun it turned everything all mud and slush so you could barely walk, and the next day the ground was again froze tight. There won't no forage for the horses, and many died and was left rotting where they fell, and they got to smell awful. The men tried to cook for themselves on open fires, but all they had was some flour and water to make a coarse bread they called firecakes. And just getting that flour was hard enough. The General sent his officers out into the countryside to try to buy flour and pork or most anything else from the local farms, but they found the British was out from Philadelphia doing the same thing – and they was paying a lot more money. The General liked to have a fit when he hears this – our army suffering, while the people he was supposed to be fighting for was selling to the enemy. On top of this, all kinds a sickness spread through the camp and frostbite too. I saw more toes and feet cut off than I could count. I'll tell you it was some tough winter – one I'll never forget.

But there was one thing all the cold and snowstorms did I was glad about. Since you could hardly even open a door to go outside, we all spent a lot of time inside and I finally found the words to ask the General some things I'd been saving up. I guess I got brave because I hear them all talking about slave soldiers again. This officer from Rhode Island tells the General he can raise an all-black battalion of soldiers from his state if only he can offer slaves their freedom. Up to that time the General would only agree to letting colored fight if they was already free, but now he has a change of heart and says okay to freeing slaves if they join the army. So one morning when we was alone I asked him how come he changed his mind 'bout this.

At first I don't know if he would say no more to me than he ever had when I questioned about black folks. But he turns to me and says, "We've got maybe fifty black soldiers out there now, and they're bleeding and starving just like the whites." He says, "They don't seem much different." I jump in and says, "So does that mean you think they're just as good at soldiering as the whites?" He don't answer at first and he seems to think about what I asked. Then finally he says, "Yes, Billy, I suppose they are."

I guess I was surprised hear him say this 'cause I almost don't say nothing back. But then I said something like, "Well, if they can be good soldiers can they be good at other things too?" He smiled at me and said, "You mean like riding a horse?" Well, I knew he was funning me 'cause he many times told me I rode as well or better than most folks white or black, or else he would never made me his huntsman back near six years before. I tell him, no, I mean more than just riding 'cause we've got good black cooks like Margaret, and there's Giles he always trusts to drive his coach, and the slave Nero he trusts with all them sheep back home. So I says, "It seems to me there's lots of black folks you think is pretty good or you wouldn't trust them with important stuff." He said, " I guess you're right about that too, Billy." But then he don't say no more so I get quiet too.

That night I talked to Margaret about what the General said. She thought the people who freed her must have begun feeling the same way – that she was a good person just like they was, and maybe they had no business owning a person. I asked her if she thought the General was thinking the same – that if black folks was good at stuff and was good people too, maybe they shouldn't be slaves? She don't know no answers more than I did – said before she was free she thought maybe God made black folks to serve white folks – said she knew lots of colored who thought maybe this was true.

I thought about what Margaret said, but I don't believe it. – A course I knew there was white people who thought that way – maybe even the General, but I can't be thinking that just by being born black it's all decided. But a strange thing happened then. It wasn't long after my talk with him about freeing slaves to fight that I hear the General and Mistress talking, and what he said made me wonder if I heard right. He tells Mistress he made a big change at Mount Vernon. He tells her he just wrote to Mr. Lund and told him he don't want him to be buying no more slaves for the plantation – and more than that, he says, "I told Lund no slaves anywhere on any of the farms are to be sold ever again."

My, oh my! I was mighty glad to learn this, 'cause he bought and sold slaves ever since I know him, and I can't help but wonder what made him change.

Chapter 12

That cold winter at Valley Forge caused two other good things – one for me, and one for the General. For me it was that I started to learn my letters. When Margaret was a girl she was companion slave to a white girl her age, and when the white girl had some schooling she would turn around and teach what she learned to Margaret. By the time she was free Margaret could read and write pretty good. Now I was learning too; she drilled me hard most every day, and by the end of winter I could make sense out of some a the words on the messages I delivered, and I was determined I would stick to it so I could some day read everything.

What was good for the General was that this Prussian man shows up in camp and says he had served some king called Frederick the Great and knew all about training men for an army. Now this was not a new thing to happen. Ever since Boston, men from over in Europe come to the General and says they want to serve in his army. Well, most of them just want to be called a colonel or a general and turns out to be more trouble than they was worth, but the General had been lucky with Lafayette so he usually at least met with these men before saying they was not a good fit. So he meets with this Prussian man who says his name is Baron von Steuben. Well, the gist of what happens is the General turns all the drilling of the entire army over to this von Steuben who drills the men all day every day and taught them army stuff they used over in Europe. The soldiers seemed to like what they learned, and by May, except their clothes still don't look so good, there was a drilled army ready to go back on the march.

And then a funny thing happens. People come out from Philadelphia with word the British is getting ready to leave the city. We can't figure out why, but then spies tell us General Howe wants to go back to England and this new Redcoat general by the name of Clinton don't think he has enough soldiers to defend the city if my General decides to attack. We was surprised to learn this 'cause as far as we knew there was way more British soldiers in Philadelphia than we had at Valley Forge, and they was a lot more fit than our soldiers. But we come to find out 8000 British and a bunch of ships was sent to a place called the West Indies. Well, I never heard of this place, but later on I learned what was going on.

It seems the big battle up at Saratoga made folks over in France think maybe we had a chance to beat the British after all – and they'd never liked the British. So they decides to join up with us and send some ships and soldiers to help. But they wasn't sending them right away to help the General. They was first going to help themselves by attacking the British in the West Indies. Well, this don't make no sense to me, but the General says the British own a bunch of islands down there where they raise sugarcane, and maybe the French would like to use this war to take those islands from them. So I ask if that means we won't see no French soldiers helping us, and the General says he don't know but he sure hoped maybe they'd help by sending us some muskets and ammunition.

A course the only Frenchman we saw for some time was Lafayette and he was already on our side, but the good thing was the British really did pull out of Philadelphia and was making like they was going to march back to New York. With all our soldiers trained by von Steuben, the General is not going to sit tight and just watch the British army go off. He sets out after them and we catch up with them at a place called Monmouth Court House in New Jersey. The generals all meet like they always do to plan the battle. General Greene was for the plan, and I'm glad 'cause I know he's got black men in his regiment all trained by that von Steuben. General Lee was loud against the plan, but the General likes it and tells General Lee what he's supposed to do and tells the others the same.

We was on this high ridge when all our generals attacked from a bunch of different places. But it wasn't one of them times when anybody was surprised. The British was ready and the fighting turned pretty fierce. General Lee was suppose to hold his position and if he needed help he was to let the General know and he would send him more troops that was held back until the General could see where they was needed most. Well, the General is watching the battles through his spyglass and all of a sudden he sees a bunch of our solders have turned tail and are running away from the British. A course he right away spurs Nelson and goes down there to see what's happening with me following along as usual. General Lee comes up riding hard with all his dogs barking and coming up behind him. The General asks, "What's the meaning of this?" and General Lee can barely talk and acts all confused. The General wants to know why Lee has left the field of battle, but he don't get no answer he likes and proceeds to let out with cursing and hollering at General Lee like I never before heard from him. He shouts, "You damned poltroon!" And says some other stuff I can't make out. I never heard him so mad and, he just whirls Nelson away, waves his sword and proceeds to try to stop the retreat.

Well, it was just like I seen so many times before. The men see the General in the lead racing all around and giving commands, and he gets them reorganized. They turn around and rush headlong behind the General and give the British soldiers a licking.

It won't no easy battle though. It was a big battle, lasted most of the day and there was lots of men killed and wounded on both sides. Toward nightfall the two armies kind of seemed like they had enough and stopped fighting to tend to their wounded. That night I knew the General was just hankering to get back at the battle, but a funny thing happened. General Clinton real quiet like sneaks his army away and by daybreak they was gone – just like maybe he learned this trick from the General. I was glad – 'cause there'd been enough killing – but I sensed the General would've been happy to keep fighting.

Them battles at Monmouth Court House in that hot summer of '78 was the last of the big battles we was to see for more than two years. The main British army stayed in New York and the General decides to divide his army and kind of surround the city. Some of our troops he put in New Jersey, some up the Hudson Valley, and some in Connecticut. He was still hoping some French ships would come to help – and a few did, but their officers don't seem too keen on attacking the British. Things settled down, the Congress comes back to Philadelphia, and the General decides it's safe to have Mistress come and settle there. So we go down to visit her a time or two. One of those times he surprises me and buys me two new coats, two new waistcoats and a new pair of breeches. I was right proud to look so good – course I know I'm really just part of how the General wants to present his own self. And I don't mind at all 'cause it was to my benefit too. But, you know, I come to see he was right about always dressing so fancy and sitting tall on Blueskin when we come into Philadelphia or any other town. People took pride in having a man who looked so good as their leader – kind of made them feel better about the war and all the tough times.

When the General decides to leave Philadelphia and go back to the army he left in New Jersey, Mistress decides to come back with us. We stayed at this place called Middlebrook that was much finer than the place at Valley Forge, and Mistress likes it enough so that she jumps right in and starts having her way. She had all her usual servants but my Margaret is still the main cook so I had it pretty good that winter, and had time to study my reading and even starts to learn to write. But there was plenty to do 'cause Mistress was going to have her socials and dinners with the other officers and their wives. She even had dances and found room to have this one dance – must have been about seventy people. I think the dances made the General homesick for Mount Vernon, but I could see he did enjoy the dancing – and all the ladies seemed to think he was pretty good. Such as this kept all us servants busy most that winter – but it was sure better than being shot at.

Chapter 13

I shouldn't make like all the General did was socialize. He still had to make sure all the soldiers had better food and shelter than the winter before at Valley Forge. But the other officers knew how to do things better now, and the army won't cooped up all in one place and could forage more for food and stuff. Also the General knew how to build those huts now and told the officers to make sure the men built them right – and he said no more dirt floors – said they caused colds and sickness – which a course made my ears ring when he says it. And he still has his spies report information and try to figure out what the British is going to do next. That meant I'm once again shed of my turban and red coat, and carrying messages to this Culper man – sometimes going in places a bit too close to British soldiers.

Long about first of the year the General hears about a battle down in Georgia. Seems the British sent some ships and soldiers there and captured the city of Savannah. We don't have none of the Continental army down there and the local militia couldn't stop the British by themselves. So after they learn Savannah is lost I listen in on the meeting deciding if there's anything they can do about this. One of the officers, a real nice man named Colonel John Laurens is from South Carolina close to this Savannah, Georgia and says he knows that place and knows the people. Now this gets me thinking 'cause I heard that name Georgia back when I was a slave for Mistress Lee. Me and Frank won't the only ones sold back then. There was this man called a Georgian who was trying to buy slaves to take to Georgia. Men from down there been around before and whenever any of us slaves hear there's a Georgian coming around we knew what that meant. So I was perked up to listen to hear what they was talking about.

Well, they wasn't talking about buying or selling slaves. They started in about that business of freeing those slaves in Georgia if they would fight. Colonel Laurens says he can go down to South Carolina and raise a whole regiment of colored solders – thousands of them – and he bets they will fight for their freedom – and more than that he says he has forty slaves of his own down there and he'll offer them the same deal. Well, I can't tell how keen the General is about all this, but it turns out he sends Colonel Laurens to Philadelphia to see if the Congress there will go along with this. It won't too long that the General gets a letter from Colonel Laurens and finds not only does the Congress think it was a good idea, but the Colonel should go right down there and offer a thousand dollars for each slave that will fight the British.

So a couple things cross my mind. One, I'm sure no slaves is getting this thousand dollars – it will be the masters – and two where is this money supposed to come from? So I asked about this 'cause I know the General is always complaining Congress won't send him money enough to buy food and uniforms for the soldiers. I says, "How come they has money to buy slaves?"

He says to me, "It will never happen 'cause those white men in South Carolina will be afraid if they arm the slaves they will turn around and use their muskets to free the other slaves and there'll be a big war – blacks against whites." He says, "That's always what whites are afraid of in the South, and that's why slavery is a bad thing."

I tells him I don't understand 'cause he owns all those slaves himself. He kind of sighs and says it's very complicated and I probably won't understand.

Well, I figured it wasn't the time to ask more questions, but I later learned that plan in South Carolina indeed fell through – I guess for reasons like he said. I did kind of poke around asking others about that money though 'cause they was always talking about not having none. Turns out it depends on what kind of money – no one had gold or silver to buy stuff – they had lots of what they called Continentals which was paper money they said nobody wanted, and I supposed that was what they thought to use to buy those slaves.

Chapter 14

One thing I've not said nothing about and I guess I should – is Indians. There was always Indians about – looking to trade a few pelts or buy some gunpowder, or maybe catch on as a guide. I never noticed them much except maybe I felt sorry for them 'cause I knew white men, especially the officers, looked down on them just like they did people of my color. But the General was concerned about them even when they was not around. He said he knew Indians and that they could turn on you in a minute. Up in Boston he'd sometimes ride out to talk to the chiefs and he'd find a blanket or something else to spare and make gifts to the chiefs and sit down and smoke a pipe with them. At Philadelphia he even invited a bunch of chiefs to what he called a Grand Council Fire. They was sitting in this big circle and I heard him say something like, "It's my business to destroy all the enemies of these states and to protect their friends." I guess he was trying to be friendly but he also parades some of the soldiers like he did for the folks in Philadelphia, 'cause what he's really saying is we have a powerful army and it would be best not to take sides against it. But I never thought while we was in New Jersey or Philadelphia there was much to worry about from Indians.

Then I hear officers talking about these six tribes up in New York State that might cause trouble. The General says they called themselves the Six Nations and been around since even before any white men crossed the ocean, and never had taken to the notion that whites could own land and keep them off. He says Indians thought nobody could own land – it was there for everyone to hunt on, and these Six Nations even made a peace with each other that lasted for hundreds of years. Well, this kinda made sense to me, so that night I asks him what was wrong with that way of thinking. He said there won't nothing wrong with thinking like that or living like that except white settlers would never stop trying to own land. He says treaties with Indians don't mean nothing 'cause there's no way to stop all the white settlers – that Indians is just temporary – whites would ignore laws and treaties and build their houses wherever they wanted. He said it was just something called destiny.

Well, I don't know nothing about this destiny business, but the General says even though Indians might be peaceful with each other, he was afraid those Six Nations would side with the British – 'cause the way he explained it, it was our people who kept moving onto Indian lands and settling there, while British soldiers just built forts and traded with them.

He was right 'cause it won't long before the trouble began. He got word this Iroquois nation attacked a settlement up in New York killing about forty settlers and taking scalps. One report even said the Iroquois made a big fire and roasted some people. A course the General is pretty upset about these stories and all the more when he hears the British put the Iroquois up to it. Over the next couple a weeks a bunch of chiefs from up there come to talk with the General to say they had nothing to do with this massacre, and they want to live in peace with the settlers. But he don't believe them – says they'll do this again unless he does something about it.

I thought he meant we would be taking some of the army and marching up there ourselves, but he says he's already got a general up there by the name of Sullivan. I see him writing this letter to General Sullivan but I don't know what orders he's sending. A few weeks later I hear what happened, and I guess it was because General Sullivan had followed orders. The army up there destroyed about thirty villages and burned all the Indian crops they could find. Maybe more than a thousand Indians was killed and the women and children not killed had no place to go and no food to eat. The General and all the other officers thought General Sullivan had taught those Indians a lesson they'd never forget.

Chapter 15

When I think back to those days I can scarcely sort out one winter from another. All I can say is it seemed like they kept getting worse. We was back in Morristown, I think for the third winter, and that time just might of been worst of all. Snow piled up as high as a house – soldiers freezing trying to dig us out. Thing is, them winters was so long. A body can take being cold for a while, and you can take having to be shut up inside – but it was weeks and months of cold, and snow, and just dismal dark days. The General did his usual best to provide for the troops, and it seems to my memory the Congress did their usual nothing to help. I was always surprised when spring come there was still any kind of army left.

I remember seeing the General real worried about losing Charleston, South Carolina when that big British fleet went down there, and I remember how angry he was that the French sent so few men and those that came don't seem to want to fight. But his main sorrow after that long winter came down to one man – and he won't even British.

There was this fort up on the Hudson River that was suppose to be the place could stop British ships from cutting off New England from New York. The General thought it was so important he sent one of his best and hardest fighting generals up there to be in charge. It was General Arnold who'd been serving the Continental army ever since we was up in Boston and he led that expedition up to Quebec – most five years before – and was wounded up there and then got another really bad leg wound at Saratoga in '78. The General thought most highly of him, and thought he was just the man to go up to West Point and make sure things was right.

This was spring or maybe summer of '80 and we was everyday on the road traveling and checking on things. I remember General Wayne's army was in pretty good shape in Connecticut, and at last the General met with the

Frenchman Rochambeau in Newport, Rhode Island, and after a bunch of toast and dinners they talked some about fighting, but I don't think nothing much came from whatever their plans was. Then we rode up to West Point to see how General Arnold was getting on. When we get there, I don't think much of it and was told to wait outside and tend the horses while the General and some other officers go inside the fort. They won't inside long when the General comes out sort of upset and says General Arnold's not there, and worse the General don't like the looks of the fort either. Says it don't look prepared for nothing. Says he talked to Arnold's wife and she seemed most anxious about seeing him and maybe General Arnold would be back tomorrow. Seemed a bit strange but I don't think too much of it until we come back the next day.

Just as we get to the fort these three militiamen ride up with a prisoner they has all tied up. They says they think he's a British soldier dressed up like a civilian, and then they show the General these papers they say the man was carrying. The General looks at the papers and I can see from the look on his face something is mighty wrong. Turns out these papers was a plan of the fort and showed where everything was – cannon, ammunition, supplies, how many troops there was – everything. The General knows only one man could have written these papers and it was General Benedict Arnold. He rushes in the fort, but a course General Arnold won't there and he says Mrs. Arnold was acting even more crazy than the day before. He later finds out General Arnold had fled across the river to the British side.

The General won't angry mad like he was when General Lee turned coward, he was just so sad. It was like somebody in his family died. He couldn't understand how General Arnold could have betrayed his country, and how he don't care none about the faith the General had in him.

I was sorry about all this but there's nothing I could do or say. Arnold was a traitor, and it was up to the General to figure what to do. Some days later spies said General Arnold was now a British General and having a gay time in New York with all the money the British give him for switching sides. Now this does get the General mad. He calls some men in and says he wants to kidnap Arnold and have him brought to him – but not to kill him. They bring this big soldier in by the name of Champe and he says he will volunteer to sneak into New York and pretend he's deserting our army. When the British warm up to him he will grab Arnold and bring him to the General. Everyone thinks it's a good plan and get together with Champe and figure how this kidnapping is going to work.

Well, I never seen Champe no more after this and I know they never did grab Arnold. But I hear the officers talking more about it and what they said puzzled me as much as anything I ever heard. They says it was only right that Champe was to get $300 and some land too for pretending to be a deserter – 'cause word that he had turned traitor might make his life pretty hard – 'specially if that plan to capture Arnold don't work. I guess that made sense to me, but then I heard 'bout the rest of his reward. Champe was to also get three slaves for his trouble!

I tell Margaret what I heard and we talk about this long into the night. I said, "How can this here war be about freedom and even about freeing slaves if they fight, and then still use black people as if they is no more than a hogshead of tobacco?" A course she don't know no more than I do, and we wonder if we is doing the right thing to be helping with this war. A course, I don't really have no choice – when I get down to it, for all the benefits I get from being the General's valet, I'm still just his property and I suppose I could be given to somebody or sold to them just like any other slave. Margaret says, "Well, just because I is free, I don't have no more choices than you do. If I want to eat and have a roof over my head I can't be choosy about where I work – and this here job cooking for the General is just about the best job I can get." She says maybe I should stop thinking so much and just be thankful for the life we have.

But I can't stop thinking 'bout it and remembering the General says it was too complicated for me to understand. And then more happens that makes understanding even harder. The Marquis come to see the General and has this short kind' a stocky black man with him. I seen him before tending to the Marquis' horses, but I never talked much to him. Turned out he was now the Marquis' valet. I thought the two of us might get acquainted while the generals talked. But that's not why the Marquis brought him. Lafayette wants him to meet the General. Says his name is James Armistead – says he's smart and loyal. Well, I sat up and took notice 'cause I was wondering where the Marquis is going with this. Turns out he had a plan. Now he's got this French accent so I don't always hear right what he's saying, but it's something like, "You ain't had no word from your man Champe so I got another plan." Says it would be easy for James to be a runaway slave and go and join the British army. Says we know where Arnold is so how about we let James sneak in and join his army. He says, "Maybe we can't catch the traitor, but we might get to know his plans." They starts talking about how a runaway slave with his ears open might learn a lot.

So now my head's spinning. One week they use slaves like hogsheads, now they say slaves can be spies. I'm wondering if this here James Armistead is just being made to do this spy business, but later I get him alone and ask him about it. He says, "No, I wants to do this." I tell him I don't understand and he says his master was for independence and so was he. Turns out James even asked his master to be allowed to volunteer for the army – he won't even promised freedom or nothing else. Says he's still a slave like me, and just wants to be in the army. And he says he'd do anything for General Lafayette cause he's been so good to him. I starts to thinking maybe it's not slavery I don't understand – maybe it's just people.

Chapter 16

While we was still up North in New York and Pennsylvania, there was a bunch going on down South that we only heard about little by little. For a while it looked pretty bad for our side and pretty good for General Cornwallis and his army. They was winning one battle after another until this place called Guilford Court House in North Carolina. That was where General Greene turned things around so that Cornwallis decides that maybe fighting in Virginia will be better. I guess he was right 'cause we soon heard the British was in Richmond.

I heard the General talking to Marquis Lafayette about taking some of the army down there to see if they can make trouble for Cornwallis. Funny thing was as they was making plans I hear them start talking about after the war was over what they would do. I perked up listening 'cause I knew they was worried about Virginia not having much militia and things right then don't look good, so I was surprised they could even be thinking about after the war. What made me listen even harder was 'cause they started talking about slaves.

The Marquis asks what the General thinks will happen with all the slaves after the British is licked. The General replies about what Dunmore had done and how so many slaves had run over to the British. But the Marquis says something like, "Well you got close to 5,000 in your own army, so maybe that's kind of even." But what he really wants to hear from the General is his take on all the rest of the slaves – he says maybe even a half million. He wants to know what will happen to them. The General says he don't know, it's not up to him to decide this – that the Congress will have to work it out.

I was listening hard and could hear all this as clear as a bell. The General pauses and then says something like, "My dear Lafayette you should know I do not like this slavery system. Slaves must be forced to work, and there must always be threats of punishment." He says his plantation is overburdened with all the slave children and people too old to work, but he still has to feed and clothe them. Then he says, "My dear friend, I have no idea or plan how to change this system I inherited from my forebears." The Marquis listens to all this then he says something made my heart skip a beat. He says, "I never would have drawn my sword to fight for America if I thought I was helping found a land of slavery!" The General don't say nothing about this, and I can see he don't want to talk no more about it.

Well, I guess they don't talk more about it – at least nothing I hear, and Lafayette gets sent off to Virginia. He's down there a while and sends back word it's even worse than they had heard, 'cause it was that traitor Benedict Arnold himself who invaded Richmond and burned about half the city. The Marquis don't have enough troops to stop Arnold's army, and it even gets worse when the British send troops up to Charlottesville to try to capture Mr. Jefferson 'cause he had written that Declaration of Independence, and the King wanted his head!

In the middle of hearing all the bad news, the General gets word that Rochambeau wants to talk more with him. So we rush back up to Rhode Island to meet with him. Well, after a couple years of those Frenchmen not doing much, now they tells the General their big fleet in the Caribbean just destroyed a bunch of British ships, so now the French fleet can move up to the Chesapeake Bay. The General gets word from Lafayette he's following Cornwallis in Virginia and he thinks the British army is heading north maybe to a river where it can get supplies from British ships.

All this stuff they hear makes the General and Rochambeau come up with the biggest plan of the war. The General finally agrees that driving the British out of New York is no longer so important. Maybe they can march the Continental Army all the way to Virginia and trap Cornwallis' army between them and the French fleet.

Chapter 17

Well, this plan commences a whole lot of action. The General don't want General Clinton in New York to know all our army is pulling out and headed to Virginia so he sends some troops west a bit and some north a bit and they're all to circle back and meet together near Philadelphia as soon as possible. And that's where we headed too. He says we'll be traveling fast and won't need Margaret's cooking, and some of the other servants too, and says I should take them into Philadelphia and get them settled. I knew right away where I wanted Margaret to be so I took her and the others to meet Ned Baxter, 'cause of that free black neighborhood where he lived. Ned says he can find housing for everyone and even jobs, 'cause with so many off fighting there's lots of work for everyone who's left. I was sad to leave Margaret 'cause we'd been most together for three years and she'd been a mighty good wife. I was worried I might never see her again, but I knew I had to leave, 'cause the General needed me, so I returned to him.

It was a big job moving about 13,000 soldiers and all our supplies. Sometimes we'd ride back to check on everything and the line of troops and wagons was strung out maybe ten miles or more. Every time we come to creek or river we had to figure out how to get everyone across, 'specially the cannon, and it sometime took days. The going was so slow, the General decides to leave the movement of the army to some of his officers so we can ride ahead to Mount Vernon and let the army catch up.

Well, it been six years since we'd been there, so we was pretty excited. Mistress was there to welcome the General, and his brothers came, and neighbors too. A bunch of slaves come up and gave their hurrahs too. They all had a grand time while I went up to the slave cemetery and found Onetta and Isaac's graves. They'd been marked just like Mistress told me, but they won't tended to so I pulled weeds and cleaned off the markers best I could. I sat there a while real quiet and thought about them. I cried a bit, but then I got up and started inquiring about where my brother Frank might be. Turns out he was doing fine 'cause somebody says, "Why, he's been made right-hand man at the distillery." I go down there and first I don't recognize him. He's grown maybe half a foot – a lot taller than me now – and gained about twenty pounds. I grab him by the shoulders and we laugh and hug. I was mighty glad to see him and proud of this new position he has. He chuckles and says, yes, he's making whiskey now but he still can't drink it. Told me he'd been married for several years and had two children, little boys – so I was an uncle and glad to be one.

Since we'd been gone so long from Mount Vernon I could see the plantation don't look so fine. Mr. Lund was not the General and he couldn't keep up the place like the General would've. But after all the war I seen I was not surprised 'cause most places you went you could see the war was hard on everything and everybody. But then I heard Mr. Lund and the General talk about the *Savage*. Seems the *Savage* was a British gunboat that went up and down the Potomac River blasting cannon and setting fires wherever it could and stealing from folks on both sides of the river. He says the captain of the *Savage* came to Mount Vernon and threatened to burn the mansion unless he was given supplies. Mr. Lund told the General he thought he was doing right by taking some sheep and hogs and other supplies down to the ship – said he was trying to save the mansion. But the General gets mad when he hears this and shouts to Mr. Lund, "I'd rather they'd burn the house and put the plantation to ruin rather than aid the enemy." He was mighty upset.

Well, this was all new to me and mighty interesting, but there was other stuff happened too. Seems when the *Savage* is down at the dock, about seventeen of the General's slaves run down there and get aboard. The captain says he'll take them to freedom. Well, I never knew what happened to them – whether they ever saw freedom or was just slaves for the British – but it sure opened my eyes to this slavery business. I'm with the General everyday and he's good to me – so good I almost forget he owns about 200 other people that surely ain't got it so good and might be quick to leave him.

Turned out we had three days to rest and then we joined back up with the army that was making its way across the Potomac. The General said about 4,000 French troops was in Virginia too, and we was all going to head down to this place called Yorktown.

*   *   *   *

The Marquis was right about what Cornwallis was doing. The British thought Yorktown was a good place to be 'cause it had a deep harbor and their ships from New York could supply them and even take them on board if they was wanting to go someplace else. A course he don't know the General had got his whole army down there and was taking positions all around the countryside. And he don't know the French fleet was out in the bay so no British ships could get to Yorktown. Main thing I remember before the battle was all these thousands of solders set to digging trenches and building ramparts circling all around the town. They cut down hundreds of trees and set them tight in the top of ramparts so they stuck forward with sharp points. The British could see all this and tried to stop it with cannon-fire but it don't slow them down much.

After maybe two or three weeks of digging and getting in closer, the General starts firing cannon on the part of the town where he thinks Cornwallis was hold up. The British try to break through our lines, but every time they tried they failed 'cause all our troops and the French attacked back. Colonel Hamilton led one of the attacks and the Marquis another. And another thing I remember was General Greene come up from Carolina with his Rhode Island regiment to join in the battle – and there was more black faces in that army than white. Kind of made me proud – especially when I hear they fought so good.

The British was outnumbered and in a bad place 'cause our cannon was up high and firing down and theirs was down low and could hardly reach us. It won't too many days of fighting when the British understood there was nothing much they could do except maybe starve and take more shelling from our cannon or surrender.

They held out for a while longer but then this big white flag comes out and they say they wants to give up. Well, it takes a few days to get the surrender organized, but it turns out to be a sight I'll never forget. There was this big open field and all our armies are in a big circle maybe fifty deep – about 17,000 men – all with muskets tall and gleaming in the sun. The British army – about 8,000 troops – is allowed to pass into the middle of the circle and one by one they has to lay down their muskets in these big piles – I never seen so many muskets in one place. Well, all the while they is marching in – which takes hours – there's this British band playing a tune. I hear later it was a tune called *The World Turned Upside Down,* and I'll bet that was the way it seemed to Cornwallis and the British. By the way – that Cornwallis never did show up himself at the surrender. He sent somebody else to give up his sword – so the General sent somebody else to fetch it too. I'd learned about officers and this dignity business by now so I wasn't surprised by this. Anyway, main thing was we had a big victory – but we also had us a mess of prisoners, and that's not always a good thing 'cause we has to feed them.

And there was another big problem too. There was maybe a thousand colored the General don't know what to do with. Most was British soldiers who took Dunmore up on that proclamation and been fighting with the British for some time. These the General decides will be carried away and treated just like the white British prisoners. But there was hundreds of others, children too, who'd been taken by the British when they ransacked through Virginia plantations. They was not exactly runaways and been put to work by the British. The General decides they will still be slaves and sends them off to Richmond so their owners can come and claim them. It don't sit right with me that people sort a stolen by the British would be put back in slavery. It was like victory was for some and slavery for others.

Chapter 18

I went on a sad trip right after that Yorktown battle. The General's stepson, Jacky Custis, was kind of an aide to the General, and while that battle was going on he came down with camp fever. The General asks me to look after him, keep his head cool and give him medicine called Peruvian bark, and whatever else he wants. But the boy's fever still got worse and worse. On the day of that big surrender he was kinda out of his mind and said he had to see it for himself, so me and Giles made a litter for him and carried him to where he could see it. He saw some but passed out before the end of the surrender, and we brought him back to our tent. Mistress sent word to take him to her brother's house about 30 miles away, so we put him in a coach and took him up there so she could come and tend to him. Miss Nelly was there too, but they couldn't do no more for him than I had, and after about a week the boy died. That was Mistress's last child, and I was most sorry for her. I could tell the General was sad too – and I think he felt he tried to do everything he could for that boy, but now it was too late.

Well, it turned out that Yorktown battle was the last I saw of fighting. We went back to Mount Vernon while the army marched prisoners to different places and then they was supposed to make winter quarters near Philadelphia. The General tries to get things going again on the plantation so I was mostly busy riding with him while he gave orders what to do – new swamps to drain for planting, fields to be cleared of trees, better oversight to make sure the slaves worked from sunup to sundown. He met all the children who'd been born since we went away. I saw my little nephews so cute and dear, but when the General saw all the children, most what he cared about was his new property, and maybe new mouths to feed. At least I had time to get to know my nephews and tell them stories about all I had seen. But what I remember most about those days was I got real brave and commenced a conversation with the Marquis.

The General and him was mighty close, and the Marquis spent many days at Mount Vernon. His man, James Armistead, was with him too, and we talked a lot. Turned out he really did get to do spy work and even learned some about what Cornwallis was doing before that battle at Yorktown. He said the Marquis would soon be returning to France and he was hoping maybe to go back with him and see that place. Don't know if he ever did, but I heard later he took Lafayette as his last name. I never did see him again after that visit.

Anyway, one day I was standing close by when James was saddling their horses and the Marquis comes out. He's always most polite to me and greets me kindly, so I brace up and say I remembered hearing him talk to the General about not coming over here if he knew he'd be fighting to make a slave country. I asks if he's talked more with the General about this. His face kind' a looked sad and he says the General is troubled about this slavery business too – but his thinking is different. The General says men have paid for their slaves – so they is property and you just can't take away people's property. Says, the General also worries what would happen if all the slaves was free – what would they do? Where would they live? Could they take care of themselves? Says there's a difference between field slaves and house slaves – that people like me could take care of ourselves if we was free – but what about the field slaves who don't know nothing but planting and picking. He says the General don't like slavery but don't know what to do about it.

Well, I don't say no more to the Marquis, but I talked to Frank about all he had to say, and Frank says he thinks the worst part of slavery is not knowing what will happen to his two boys. He says his life is fine, he likes his work; his wife spends her days spinning and weaving and is okay with that too. But they often talk about their boys. "They can just be taken away from us at any time," he says, "just like we was when we was young." He says that's the worst part of slavery. We talk more about it, and one thing I tell him is the

General was more hurt than mad when all those folks ran away on the *Savage*. Says they should be loyal to him 'cause he treated them right. Frank says that's the trouble with white folks – they always think of themselves as the ones who is hurt and don't care to understand how it feels to be owned by somebody. This makes me think again about what Ned said about him being more of a man than me 'cause he was free. Now I know he was right, 'cause how much of a man can you be if you can't even protect your own children?

*   *   *   *   *

After a few weeks I had to say goodbye to Frank and my little nephews 'cause the General and Mistress said we was all going back to Philadelphia. Well, I was sad to leave Frank, but most happy to hear it was Philadelphia we was going to, and I asked if when we get there can I go and fetch Margaret so she can cook for him again. I thought maybe he even smiles a little when he says, "Yes, that would be fine."

Chapter 19

That was a mighty easy time in Philadelphia. All we had to worry about was entertaining the people who come to tell the General what a great man he was and how he done made the country. He was honored with songs about him, bands striking up music to honor him, people coming in to paint his portrait, and it seemed like every night there was dinner parties somewhere in the city. Margaret did her share of the cooking, but the General brought in this Frenchman who was kind of in charge.

I liked Philadelphia 'cause I got to be with Margaret, and we had free time enough so both of us got to go visit Ned and Francie and their little family a time or two, and visiting where he lived was what I liked best about that city. There was so many free colored going about their business and acting like they was as good as anybody – made me wonder if the General don't see this too. Me and Ned walked around his neighborhood and he told me all the jobs people had, money they was making, and that there was even laws in the city that protected black folks like him. I asked like what, and he says like owning property – he was buying the house where he lived with Francie – and it was legal and no one could take it away. Says there was this Free African Society starting schools for colored all over the city, and that one he told me about before, run by the Quakers, was still there too.

By now I was more comfortable asking the General about things, and he won't near as busy, so one day I tell him some of the stuff I learned from Ned, and asked if he don't think it was a good thing. He says he knows Philadelphia was different from Virginia and Mount Vernon – says he even knows there is more than 6,000 free Negroes in the city, and no one much seemed to be complaining about them. But he says he don't know what would happen if the plantations just turned loose their slaves – said they couldn't all just come up to Philadelphia, and they couldn't just start up a new city.

Then he surprises me and says more. He goes on to tell me what the Marquis had said to him. Said Lafayette wanted to buy a farm and do an experiment with slaves – said Lafayette's idea was to free them and treat them like tenants. Said they'd be taught to do all the chores on a farm and how to run a farm, not just learn to pick cotton or plant tobacco. The General said maybe it would be an idea for after there was a peace with England.

I was amazed he talked to me like this, and I said, "What about people like me – we never got experience with farming – we been trained to serve white folks in mansions. What can house servants do if we be free?"

He says he supposes we could get paid and keep right on doing what we is doing. Then he looked at me kind of funny and says, "Is that what you want, Billy? You want to be paid?"

I tell him, "No, I is happy just the way things is, and I know I have a special place with you. I never leave your service, pay or not." But I also tell him, "The more I seen of this country riding around with you, the more I think there don't need to be slaves. This whole slavery business is not right – black people can never decide stuff for themselves, never know what will happen to their children, never be real men, never be equal like that document says."

I never talked my mind like that to him before, but I could see he listened to me and don't seem angry. But he don't say nothing – he just sighs and makes up something for me to do so we don't have to talk no more about it.

Well, it would've been just fine with me to stay in Philadelphia, but the General says the British army is still in New York, so we best pull our army together and go back up there. We make the long ride up to Newburgh up on the Hudson River – and find a big farmhouse. There's room for the house servants, but the General wants the French cook and says there won't be room for another cook, so I had to tell Margaret she'll have to stay in Philadelphia again. I get her settled with Ned and the Methodists and I think she'll be fine.

Since he's still got his army, the General tells Rochambeau he still wants to drive the British from New York. I'm thinking to myself maybe he's stuck on this 'cause that was his worse defeat in the war, and he wants to make up for it. But the French general don't agree, and without the French navy, the General knows he don't have a chance to take New York. I listen to them talk and wonder what the General will do with his army. One day I hear him talking to Colonel Hamilton about what Dr. Franklin and Mr. Adams has been doing the past couple years. Seems they been over in France and talking with some men from England too. Talk was maybe them British thought they was losing too many big battles and it was costing too much to keep fighting. Colonel Hamilton says they was talking about how to end this war with a treaty. But I don't hear no more right then.

Main reason why Colonel Hamilton was there was the grumbling in the army. He says the troops think if there does come a peace they won't no need no army – that the men will be sent home before they gets the pay they are owed – and maybe won't ever get it. It sounded to me like the same old story since the beginning of the war – broken promises to the troops. But this time Colonel Hamilton says it's worse 'cause it's the officers who are grumbling now. They been promised salary and land too, and ain't received none. The Colonel says these men know a peace means they would put down their weapons and they don't want to do this until they gets what they is supposed to. They say the Congress is too weak to make the states pay up what they owe and maybe if that Congress can't do what it should, the army should just take over the country – and the General should be in charge of everything.

The General is mighty upset when he hears this. He tells the Colonel to set up a meeting so he can talk to the officers. Colonel Hamilton quick arranges this big meeting in

Newburgh and spreads word the General wants all the officers there. I see him at his writing desk all night long writing the speech he wants to make to them, and he seems mighty worried. That night when he gets there to make the speech I can see most of the officers is upset – some even seem hostile. I'm off to the side so I can't make out everything the General says, but I can make out he tells them he has been their faithful friend through eight years of war – he's always been on their side. He struggles with his glasses and says he has gone grey and is growing blind in their service and would never desert them. Some of the men has tears in their eyes as they listen to him, and when he says if they take up arms against the Congress they will destroy everything they have been fighting for, I can see the fight has gone out of most of the officers.

A few weeks later I hear that treaty they was talking about was signed over in France and it means the war will be over and British soldiers will go back to England. They say this treaty says where the boundaries of America will be, tells when the British solders will leave Charleston and New York, tells who can fish in which waters, and tells what to do about prisoners.

Well, a course I knows this is good news and all this is important to the General, but it's what else they talk about that I care most about. I hear the treaty also says if the black British soldiers was runaway slaves, they is to be returned to their masters. The General seems to think this is okay – and I'm sorry to hear him say so. The Marquis and Colonel Hamilton says this would be a wrong thing to do, but I hear the General say he's even fixing to send a man looking for his own runaways from when they went on the *Savage*. I was thinking his talking to me about how bad slavery was must have just been talk.

Well, it took months for the General and the British generals to work out everything. The British had been in New York for seven years and won't in no hurry to leave. Lots of Tories was there too, and was thinking they'd better leave too before it was known they aided the enemy. Lots of them Tories had done pretty well for themselves during the war, so not everybody was happy about that peace treaty. The General finally works it out so the British would leave sometime in November – it was 1783 – eight and a half years since we rode off to war.

The General decides we should be in New York for when the British leave, but it was slow getting there 'cause every town we traveled through had parades for the hero and big celebrations and dinners, and even fireworks. Places wanted him to stay for days so he could shake hands with seemed like everyone in the town.

We finally get to New York and march in with a small army – maybe 800 men – and I hear some cheering – and some people real quiet – and I hear this one woman say she can't believe this is the army that won the war 'cause the soldiers is so poorly dressed. I can see myself when the British soldiers march out to board their ships they still look mighty sharp all in their bright red uniforms. But they done lost and we won so it don't matter much.

One thing I'm glad to see is the black British soldiers is leaving too. This was one time the General don't get his way. I heard the British General told him he don't care what that treaty said – he gave his word to his black soldiers they would have their freedom, and when the white troops was loaded on ships he made sure the black soldiers went with them. I hear they went to this place up in Canada called Nova Scotia.

Then it was time for the General to say his goodbyes to the officers and troops. They picked this place called Fraunces Tavern to have this big dinner and make all the toasts. Mostly they was waiting for the General to say his last words to them, but he seemed kind of shaken and choked up. He said his heart was filled with love and gratitude – and I surely understood this 'cause so many of the men had stayed with him through all the hard times. The men all cheered for the longest time, and I could see many never wanted to see him go.

But we did leave and a few weeks later we was in Annapolis 'cause that's where the Congress was, and the General had to go through the goodbyes all over again. This time he was resigning his commission as commander-in-chief of the Continental Army. They had another big dinner with toasts and all that, but the real ceremony was the next day at the State House, and it was real quiet like. I heard men whisper there was never nothing like it. They said the General was a hero and could be king. But the General wanted no part of that, and said he was no more the head of the army and the Congress was in charge. I could tell it was a big deal and why people thought it was maybe even amazing he don't want to be king. But I know maybe what they don't – all the General wants to do is go home to Mount Vernon and be left alone.

Chapter 20

We get to Virginia in time for Christmas 'cause the General promised Mistress he would. I won't so happy as the General 'cause Margaret had not been with us for most a year, and he was in such a hurry to get to Mount Vernon he don't stop at Philadelphia so I can see her. When I see how happy the General is with all his family, it makes me a bit lonesome. I know Margaret was doing fine, 'cause she was working for the same folks as before and I know Ned and Francie looked after her, but I still missed her. I asked the General about bringing her to Mount Vernon to be his cook and I got pretty excited 'cause he said next time we was up that way we'd bring her back!

In the meantime, since my little nephews was about six and seven, I thought it would be time to teach them to ride, and the General said that would be fine. Most of the horses had been used for the army but there was a fine colt yearling that I broke for the saddle, and set to teach the boys to ride. Junus was the oldest, and he took to horses just like I did as a boy. Frankie junior wasn't so sure, and shied away at first – never did warm up to horses like Junus, but later he learned to ride and care for horses good enough so he could groom them if called to do so. Junus rode so good I even had the General come out and watch him. Frank was happy I could spend so much time with the boys 'cause he had twelve hour days at the distillery, and was always tired when he got home at night.

I thought we'd be staying at Mount Vernon for a while 'cause the General still had so much to do to get the plantation right again, but come spring he's ready to be off doing something else. Maybe it was all the company made him want to leave, 'cause it was worse than before the war. It was like Mount Vernon was a big tavern – strangers thought they should just come to see the General and then stay as long as they liked. The house servants and cooks did best they could, but sometimes I don't think there was enough hogs and chickens in ten miles to feed everyone who showed up. And they thought their horses should be fed too. I seen the forage bins near empty several times.

Well, anyway whether it was the crowds of people or whatever, come fall the General organizes this group of men and we was off to Ohio country. He had land there – lots of it – and there was tenants living on his land for years and not paying rent. I never crossed mountains before and I don't care if I never do again. It was rough traveling and I couldn't help wonder why the General don't just send somebody else to take care of those tenants. Maybe it was 'cause this was the country he first explored back when he fought the French and Indians, and I could see he enjoyed seeing mountains and rivers he knew from back then.

A couple things was different from all our travels back east. These Indians out there was never happy with all the settlers coming on their hunting grounds. The General said this was the same as when he was there thirty years before leading the Virginia militia back before I knew him. Well, now the General don't have no army to teach those red men who was boss. In fact, there was some places we was scared to go through 'cause of talk of killings and kidnappings by Indians. The other thing different was those white settlers don't care much who the General is. Maybe news don't get out there and these folks don't hear what he done. There was no folks calling him "Your Excellency," and some was downright hostile especially when he says they must get off his land. I never seen people disrespect him before – so I was kind of surprised.

The General says he would sue to have tenants removed from his land or they had to pay the rent they owed. He says this land had to be developed by people who respected the law and he would try to make this happen. He even talks about having canals built so more people can come and make settlements and towns. Said this would drive the Indians further west and cause civilization to spread. Well, I don't know if this is just talk 'cause I don't know what the future holds, but my own future don't look so good 'cause of what happened on our way back over the mountains.

The General had this big piece of land on the Kanawha River he says never been surveyed properly, and he wants to do it now. Well, I never been surveying, but he has all his old surveying equipment with him and gets busy setting up his scope and telling everyone what to do. He tells me to climb over yonder rocks and carry this surveying chain. It's heavy, but not so heavy I can't carry it, and I'm climbing on the rocks pretty careful 'cause they is slippery. Next thing I know my feet slip out from under me and I come down hard on one knee. I never felt so much pain. Learned later I broke what they call the knee pan. The General has to fetch a sled, and for two long weeks I was dragged through the maintains, and then laid in a wagon all the way back through Virginia to Mount Vernon.

Turns out I was laid up for most half a year. I tell the General I'd be most pleased if he would send for Margaret up in Philadelphia and have her come care for me. He says that's a right good idea so I tell the General she goes to that black Methodist church, and tell what I know about getting around the city to where Ned lives. He says he'll write this man he knows in Philadelphia named Clement Biddle and have him arrange for Margaret's travel. After a few weeks he hears from this man Biddle who says he can't find Margaret – says he couldn't even find Ned, say no one knows where they are; so he stops looking.

Well, I don't understand this and I don't know how hard anybody really looked. But the General tried to do for me and I don't think I can question him, so I just stay in bed and gets sadder everyday. I suppose I was lucky to be cared for each day and know I was treated better than any slave could expect – but it don't help much with how I feel inside.

One thing I hear while I'm laid up, and I had to ask the General about it. We end up having more conversation than ever before. I hear the General talking to some man named

Lawson about buying his slave, a man named Neptune. Well, I remembered hearing him say he told Mr. Lund never to buy no more slaves, and I'm wondering if now that the General's back running things if he's changed his mind. He talks to me about it and says this is special 'cause he needs a good bricklayer, and this Neptune is supposed to be one of the best.

I said, "It just seems funny to me that to get a good brick layer you have to own a man. All them states we traveled through up North, people need work done they just hires a man to do it. I'll never understand this business of owning people."

He said, "Being up North maybe put notions in your head that don't work in Virginia."

I said, "General, I understands life on this plantation – I knows you got lots of work to be done and needs slaves to do it. I know you try to treat them right, and I do understand it's complicated to try to figure how to change it all. But it don't make no sense to me that you get better work when you own a man than when you hire him for pay. What if he don't work good? If you own him, you're left to feed and clothe a poor worker. If you hires him, you can just let him go if he don't work good."

The General says, "Billy, it seems you understand better than I thought. And if that's so, I'm sure you've seen I must constantly enforce work rules to get my slaves to give a full day's work. It's not a good system – and for more reasons than you know. It's almost impossible to find hard working white men because our society insists black slaves must do the work. And many whites, rich in land and the labor of slaves, fool themselves by thinking this system will last. I can change none of this – and as for Neptune I still need a good bricklayer, and if I don't buy him and instead rent him from Mr. Larson, Neptune will still be a slave. It will not change a thing."

A course he was right. There was nothing much nobody could do. Traveling and learning all about this slavery business and understanding how it worked, and even years a thinking hard about it, don't matter much at all.

Chapter 21

While I was laid up, the General has to have a new valet, and even after I'm walking again, I can't really do a full day, so he gives me a new job. He's got three men do nothing all day but make shoes, belts, and other things of leather. I know all of them from back before the war, and know they was good men – worked hard. But the General says they need to be supervised and I should do it. I says, "What should I do?" He says, "Just make sure they work all day." Well, I knows what he was doing – he's just giving me a job where I can sit most of the time, and maybe be out of the way so folks won't see me so favored.

It's a pretty easy job 'cause we're all friends, and they teach me how to do some cobbling too, and I gets fairly good at it. At least I learn to make shoes good enough for the field slaves – never learned to make fine ones for the house servants though – and only one man – name of Bemus, made shoes fine enough for white folks. The General bought his from England just like before the war, with mighty fine buckles.

Time went by and I was well enough to help the house servants when there was special guests – and turned out they was truly special 'cause they was to be big names later on. This little man – about my size really – named Mr. James Madison come several times, Colonel Hamilton was there, and Mr. James Monroe too. I hear them talking that if something's not done this new country won't be no more and there'll just be thirteen small ones, just like when we was colonies. Seems there's fighting up in Massachusetts with farmers against the militia, lots of soldiers still not paid, the French mad because we ain't paid our debts, and all those countries over in Europe won't even talk with our people 'cause they say we're not really a country.

A course this means the General has to do something – says he fought too long to make America and don't want it to fall apart. So it's just like ten, twelve years before, they decides there'll be a big meeting in Philadelphia and try to get all the states to send people to decide how to be a real country.

I tell the General I'm well enough to travel and be his valet again, but he's not sure. His new man, Paris, has been doing just fine, so I'm not really needed. He sees I'm dearly disappointed not to be with him and says well maybe he needs two good men. I'm surely happy about this and before long there's four of us off traveling again – Giles driving the coach, Paris leading Nelson, and me leading Blueskin. Traveling through towns is just like before – people wants to see the General so he gets out of the coach and rides one or the other of his favorite horses through the towns and then he's back in the coach.

We finally gets to Philadelphia, but it's been four years and the city's not the same no more – not so crowded, not so busy, and mostly – no Margaret. I look for her, and Ned too. Still no word about Margaret – it's like she just disappeared. I talk to maybe a hundred people, but nobody knows nothing about her. She was from up near Boston, so I think maybe she somehow went up there, but I never found out. I do learn that Ned and Francie moved on to New York 'cause since the war ended there's not much work in the shipyards no more.

As for the General, Philadelphia meant he was always on parade. Everywhere we went big crowds followed. If he just walked down the street, mobs of people would just kind a swallow him up so you could hardly see him. We would get away from the crowds by taking rides early in the morning. And the General still wants everybody with him to look good and buys me a special black handkerchief to wear around my neck and new breeches and stockings too.

Well, the General spends his days in the State House with all the others, and a course everyone now knows what those famous men talked about all those hot summer days in 1787. It turned out to be the Constitution of the United States and it was most important 'cause it was to fix the problem of the states being so separate and make a real country. And even though we don't know it then, while me and Paris and Giles was waiting around outside they was also talking about what to do with all us slaves.

We soon found out they talked a lot but really don't do nothing much 'cept say we only count as part of a person. Sounded funny – but none of us was too surprised by this 'cause we long ago learned our place – and a course, we know our place won't so bad and it don't much bother us what they did.

But then we talk about this real quiet, and get sad for all our slave brothers and sisters. We know what many a their lives was like – robbed of liberty, starved or beaten just 'cause somebody wants to, and maybe raped by masters. The words in that Independence document they used to make so much fuss over don't seem to matter now when it come making a country. We talked about how over the years of war we met a lot of the men that was in that meeting hall – Dr. Franklin, Mr. Adams, Colonel Hamilton, Mr. Madison – all good men. Giles said something was as true then as it is now these twenty odd years later. He says, "You know, if all these great men – best men their states can send – can't figure out what's right by us, I guess it'll be a long time 'fore there's any changes do right for any black man."

There was nothing else to say.

Chapter 22

Well, we all went back to Mount Vernon and the General was busier than ever 'cause all these important men was meeting with him most every day about that new Constitution. Seems the states had to vote for it before it would mean anything, and I guess there was lots of folks against it 'cause the General seemed mighty worried it won't pass. One day when nobody's with him and he don't seem too occupied I says to him, "I hears that Constitution says black men is only part of a man."

He looks up at me and tries to explain it to me, but the only thing I understand is men in the South who has all the slaves wants them all counted so their states has more power, and men in the North says slaves shouldn't count at all 'cause they ain't free men. So the General says they did something called a compromise and that slaves would count as part of a man – a little more than half.

Still don't make no sense, but I says to him, "I guess it don't really matter none. Why should all those famous men care 'bout us slaves?"

He pulls off his glasses and thinks a minute, like he's wondering whether he should talk more about it. Then he says, "Billy, we just couldn't do anything about slavery. Every time somebody tried to talk about some way slaves might be free, the Carolina and Georgia men said they'd walk out if there was any talk of freeing slaves."

I says "So it just goes on forever – my little nephews and all the other children don't ever even have a chance to be free?"

He says, "I'm afraid that's right; the convention didn't address the issue of freedom at all." Then he kinda thoughtful like says, "Maybe time will tell about the folks I own here at Mount Vernon, we'll just have to wait and see."

Well, we don't talk no more about it, and a course everybody knows the Constitution did pass, and it makes my General president. I know this was big – kind of like a king – but with others picked to help. I tell him I was right proud and should I start calling him "Your Excellency" like most everybody was doing now. He says, "No, 'General' will still be just fine."

Then just when we starts packing for the trip to New York for the inauguration and celebration, I had another fall. I was riding to the post office in Alexandria City, when Chinkling slips on some ice and we both end up on the ground. He falls on my good leg, and the upshot is I then had two bad knees and again couldn't walk none. The General has me taken care of like before, but I'm still not better when it's time to make the trip to New York.

I says to him I really wants to go and keep serving him now he's President, but he says I'm probably not healed enough to be of much use. I keep after him, and finally he says yes I can come, and I was mighty glad. Well, I still can't ride, so he has me in a coach. First, when we set out I'm doing all right, but by the time we get to Philadelphia I'm in so much pain I can't travel no more. The General has to go on, but he has his man Clement Biddle take care of me – fact this good man has this steel brace made for my leg, and doctors see me most every day.

Well, there was some talk 'bout putting me on a ship back to Alexandria, but I says, "I feel much better and still wants to go to New York to serve the General." Mr. Biddle says there's three flights of stairs in the mansion where the General lives and I can't be of no use. But I asks him to write the General and ask him if I can come. I guess the General still thought I could help 'cause he sends word, "Yes, send Billy on." So before too many days I was on this ferryboat and on my way. Sad to say, I don't get there in time for the inauguration ceremony, but I stayed and worked in the mansion best I could.

It won't like before 'cause he's got Paris and Giles and a new man, Hercules, there to help, and some others too. The General made sure we was all dressed splendidly, just like he always wanted his house servants, but now even more. I couldn't leave the house much, but Giles and Paris had ruffles on the sleeves and fine new stockings and hats – all fancy stuff whenever they went with the General. But even though everybody in those times was dressed up and formal like, and surely treated the General with great respect, I don't think he was happy. It won't like at Mount Vernon or back in the army when the General says, "Do it!" and people jumped. From what I could see, Presidents is supposed to listen to folks, write a bunch of letters, and do that compromising business. Maybe the servants could be commanded, but it seemed to me most folks just talked. I guess making a government is hard, and the General seemed like he grew older every day.

We was only in New York for about a year and a half when we was off again to Philadelphia. Seems it was one of those compromises that changed where the capital was to be, and I guess it made some folks happy for it to be in Philadelphia. The General decides since he has to move he wants a bigger place so he can bring even more servants up from Mount Vernon. Mistress comes up too, with her own coach and servants. There's so many of us we spread out – some in the attic, some in what used to be a smoke house, and others in a whole house just for servants. There's more than twenty, and new people I don't know. Hercules is trained to be the cook and the General is mighty pleased with him, and I'm told I should train this new boy named Christopher to be personal valet, and I'm not sorry, 'cause my knees is worse and worse most every day.

Problem I don't think the General thought about happens when he brings all these servants to Philadelphia. He learns about this Pennsylvania law, says if a slave lives in the state for six months, he's a free man. Well, I never heard this either, but many white folks is serious about this abolition business, and lots more maybe is worried about it. The General says since he is President this law don't count for him, but others is not so sure about this. And I know the General is thinking he treats all of us so well nobody would ever leave him. A course that's true for me, but I don't know about everyone else.

And it's not just the General worried about this. All the men from the South who has slaves up there is worried. So what they starts to do is send their servants home every six months for a while, then bring others in, and have the first group come back later. Well, I knew what was going on, and the General decides maybe he should do this too. But he tries to hide why he is sending folks back and forth, like it's just natural to be sent on errands and such. And to tell you the truth, servants mostly just do as we is told, so if that's what we is supposed to do, most do it. But he has these two that is not so sure.

I don't know the whole story 'cause truth was I wasn't long able to do much good up in Philadelphia. After about a year I was sent back here to be the overseer of the house servants – and I was mighty pleased the General thought so good of me to give me this position. It's an easy job 'cause everybody here knows what to do and does it, and with the General and Mistress up in Philadelphia there's hardly no company, so we're really just minding the place. But one day Hercules comes back by coach from Philadelphia all upset 'cause he says the General don't have trust in him. He says to me, "The General sent me back – thinks if I stay in Philadelphia I'll try to take my freedom and won't serve him no more." Turns out Hercules is told to stay here for a week, then he's given money to take the stage back to Philadelphia. And he's mighty upset at not being trusted.

I tells him this slavery business is complicated. We is always trusted to run errands here and there, we carry money to pay for stuff, and is given fine horses, or ride in coaches that can take us anywhere. So our masters must know for years we don't run off and they don't suspect we will. But when someone says we might be free they gets all upset. I tell Hercules not to worry about it – that's just the way it is and pretty soon I know he'll be back in Philadelphia cooking for the General again. A course I was right, and Hercules ended up as a mighty fine cook up there for another six years.

But there was this other girl, too. Mistress has this servant girl named Oney. She's been fixing Mistress's hair and being body servant for a while now. I know Mistress is fond of her, just like she was of my Onetta years back. Well, Oney likes her work and wants to stay with Mistress – now this is years later when the General is fixing to come back here for good. Oney tells him she'll come back but she knows she can say she is free 'cause she's lived in Philadelphia for so long. Well, I don't learn how this works out until Mistress and the General is back home and Oney's not with them. Turns out Oney said she'd only come back as a free woman. Well, this was the wrong thing to say to the General – he wants her back, but no one's going to make the terms of any agreement except him – so he can't say Oney is free, and Oney leaves and goes to New York, and nobody sees her no more.

My General's a good man – I knows this and seen him good to people over the years – but he's just like all the other slave owners when it comes to letting servants be free. He can't see many of us would still be glad to serve as before if only it would be our own choice to do so. I don't know if he would ever understand being free makes you a whole man.

Epilogue

I had listened to William Lee each day for three weeks as he told his story. But after his last description of General Washington, he seemed to be talked out. He said, "Well, that's about it, now you've heard my whole story." I'd hardly prompted him along the way, but now I wanted to know more – it seemed his story needed an ending. I asked him if there wasn't more he could tell about the last years of the General's life. He said, "Well, I don't have no more adventures with the General – truth was I don't serve him at all when he returned. There won't much I could do with these bum knees, and Mistress looked after all the house servants herself, so I went to live with Frank and his family."

I asked if that was a good time for him. He said, "Sure, a great time. Frank and his wife Sally made my days comfortable and I was able to spend most days with Junus and Frankie junior. They was good boys, and better and better with horses so I get the General to let them work full-time at the stables. I sits and watch them ride, especially Junus, and give points how to ride low and tells about jumping over hedgerows and ducking British musket balls. Pretty soon seems all I'm doing is reliving those war days 'cause so many folks come by and wants to hear my stories."

I said, " Billy, you've been free now for ten years. General Washington freed you in his will. Have you changed your opinion of how he treated his slaves?"

"Well, like the General always said, it's complicated." Billy thought a minute then contimued, "Sure I'm free and well provided for. I can live out my life here at Mount Vernon and never need a thing – and a course I'm mighty grateful to the General for this. And I suppose you knows that when Mistress died all of the General's slaves get their freedom too. But do you know about the others?"

I told him I just assumed all the Mount Vernon slaves were freed by General Washington's will. Billy said, "No, that's what most people think too, but Mistress got near 200 more slaves that go to her grandchildren. It's George Washington Parke Custis who owns her slaves. They is now his slaves."

We had not heard this up North, and I was somewhat startled to learn the truth. I asked Billy, "So how many slaves were actually freed?"

He said, "Near as I could tell about 120. And they was provided for too. The old and lame like me can stay here and gets food and clothes and mostly live as before. Under twenty-five could go to Alexandria and learn to read and write, and the General fixed it so they could leave Virginia if they wants to or stay here and get work. I heard he wrote his will so fine nobody could change it."

I asked, "What about your nephews, are they free?"

He said, "Now that's an interesting case and probably tells you as much about how slavery works as anything else. You see, me and Frank was the General's slaves cause he bought us from Mistress Lee. But when Frank married Sally, she's a Custis slave. So this law in Virginia says slaves go by the mother, and this makes Junus and Frankie be Custis slaves too. So to answer your question, no, my nephews is not free. And worse they was sold off this plantation about five years ago and I have no idea where they might be."

Billy's eyes welled with tears as he told this last sorrowful story, and I could tell he'd rather say no more. I looked at his sad wrinkled face, but remembered that during most of his discourse he seemed happy with his recollections – indeed even exuberant when he described his wartime adventures with his General. Now as he reflected on the many unsolved contradictions of slavery and its impact on those he loved, he was pensive. And certainly his sadness affected me as well. In the stillness of the moment I wondered whether this man before me actually contributed to the benevolence of his master's last will and testament.

I thanked Billy for being so generous with his time as he told his truly unique story, and I took my leave. As I rode down the well cared for lane and left Mount Vernon I certainly understood the complications of slavery Billy had described so well. What I surmise is that General Washington's instincts were against the institution, and absent conflict – his nature was caring, and his reward for loyalty obvious. But the other side of his nature could never give up a master/slave mentality – that he was owed their service until he himself decided otherwise. And certainly he was caught up with the reality that Virginia and the South are so entrenched with this institution that he could see no end to it.

As I rode back toward the Potomac, the beauty of the Virginia landscape filled my vision, but my heart ached for a country where even its founding father could not see a path toward fulfillment of its most basic creed.

Colonel Elisha Sheldon
May 29, 1809

Appendix I

Contemporaneous References to William Lee

(1) Listing of his name and price paid: "Will, 61 pounds, 15 shillings"
George Washington, "Cash Accounts," May 3, 1768, *The Papers of George Washington, Colonial Series,* 10 Volumes, edited by W.W. Abbot and Dorothy Twohig, Charlottesville: University Press of Virginia, 1983-1995), 8:82 & 83n

(2) From Lund Washington letter to George Washington, December 30, 1775 (typescript, FWS Library, Mount Vernon, VA)

"... if it will give Will any pleasure he may be told his wife and child are both very well."

(3) Quote from Dr. James Thacher cited in Ron Chernow's Washington: a Life, Penguin Books, New York, 2010, P. 359

"His Excellency, with his usual dignity (was) followed by his mulatto servant Bill, riding a beautiful gray stead."

(4) Letter from Martha Washington cited in Chernow, P. 360

"The General and Billy (Lee), followed by a lot of mounted savages, rode along the line."

(5) George Washington letter to Clement Biddle, July 28, 1784, *The Writings of George Washington,* 27:451

"The mulatto fellow William, who has been with me all the war is attached (married he says) to one of his own colour a free woman, who during the war was also of my family. She has been in an infirm state of health for some time and I had conceived that the connection between them had ceased, but I am mistaken; they are both applying to me to get her here, and tho' I never wished to see her more yet I cannot refuse his request (if it can be complied with on reasonable terms) as he has lived with me so long and followed my fortunes through the war with fidelity.

After promising thus much, I have to beg the favor of you to procure her passage to Alexandria either by sea, by the passage Boats (if any there be) from the head of Elk, or in the stage as you shall think cheapest and best, and circumstances may require.

She is called Margaret Thomas als. Lee (the name which he has assumed) and lives at Isaac and Hannah Sills, black people who frequently employ themselves in cooking for families in the city of Phila. She should be sent to Mount Vernon if it can be complied with on reasonable terms, as he has lived with me so long and followed my fortunes through the war with fidelity."

(6) From Elkanah Watson, January 1785, in Jean B. Lee, editor, *Experiencing Mount Vernon: Eyewitness Accounts, 1784-1865* (Charlottesville, VA: University of Virginia Press, 2006), 23

"His servant Billy, the faithful companion of his military career, was always at his side. . ."

(7) Clement Biddle letter to George Washington, April 27,1789, *The Papers of George Washington, Presidential Series*, 2:113

"I have frequently called to see Billy, he continues to be too bad to remove . . ."

(8) Tobias Lear letter to Clement Biddle, May 3, 1789, *The Papers of George Washington, Presidential Series*, 2:134n

"The President would thank you to propose it to Billy to return to Mount Vernon when he can be removed, for he cannot possibly be of any service here . . ."

(9) Tobias Lear letter to Clement Biddle, June22, 1789, *The Papers of George Washington, Presidential* series, 2:133

"Billy arrived here safe and well."

(10) George Augustine Washington letter to George Washington, August 20, 1790, *The Papers of George Washington, Presidential Series*, 6:311

"Sadly, Will was unable to manage the pace in the presidential household and returned to Mount Vernon in the summer of 1790."

(11) From Washington's will dated: July 9, 1799

"And to my Mulatto man William (calling himself William Lee) I give immediate freedom; or if he should prefer it (on account of accidents which have rendered him incapable of walking or of any active employment) to remain in the situation he now is. It shall be optional in him to do so: In either case however, I allow him an annuity of thirty dollars during his natural life, which shall be independent of the victuals and cloaths he has been accustom to receive, if he chuses the last alternative; but in full with his freedom, if he prefers the first; & this I give him as a testimony of my sense of his attachment to me, and for his faithful services during the Revolutionary War."

(12) George Washington Parke Custis, *Recollections and Private Memories of Washington, by his Adopted Son George Washington Parke Custis with a Memoir of the Author, by His Daughter; and Illustrative and Explanatory Notes, by Benson J Lossing, New York,* 1860, p.163

"It is very hot nearly 100 degrees, Billy Lee has assumed unofficial command of the servants and valets for all the general officers, leading them on horseback to the top of a hill beneath a large sycamore tree where they can more easily observe the looming action and catch the cooling breeze. As Billy Lee takes out his telescope to observe the battlefield, Washington looks up at the group and is heard to observe: 'See those fellow collecting on yonder height; the enemy will fire on them to a certainty.' And just as Washington speaks a six-pound artillery ball lands in the sycamore tree, scattering but not injuring Billy Lee and his fellow servants, whom the British had apparently mistaken for Washington and his staff."

(13) Custis, *Recollections and Private Memories of Washington*, p.387

"Will, the huntsman, better known in Revolutionary lore as Billy, rode a horse called Chinkling, a surprising leaper, and made very much like its rider, low but sturdy and of great bone and muscle. Will had but one order, which was to keep with the hounds: and, mounted on Chinkling, a French horn at his back, throwing himself almost at length on the animal, with his spur in flank, this fearless horseman would rush, at full speed, through brake and tangled wood, in a style at which modern huntsmen would stand aghast . ."

(14) Custis, *Recollections and Private Memories of Washington*,

Billy is said to have "received considerable largesses from the numerous visitors to Mount Vernon." P. 157

(15) Custis, *Recollections and Private Memories of Washington*,

". . . one morning Westford was sent for to bring Billy out of a fit. The blood would not flow. Billy was dead." P. 157n

Appendix 2

Glossary of Historical Events and Persons Perhaps Not Well Known

Prologue

Colonel Elisha Sheldon - The 2nd Continental Light Dragoons, also known as Sheldon's Horse after Colonel Elisha Sheldon, was commissioned by the Continental Congress on December 12, 1776. The 2nd Light Dragoons are prominent in Colonel John Trumbull's paintings of the American Revolution. (Though selected to be the scribe for William Lee's narrative, there is no record that the two men actually met.)

Chapter 1

Jumping the Broom - In some African-American communities, marrying couples will end their ceremony by jumping over a broomstick, either together or separately. This practice is well attested for as a marriage ceremony for slaves in the Southern United States who were often not permitted to wed legally. Its revival in 20th century African American culture is due to the novel and miniseries Roots.

Chapter 2

Colonel William Byrd - William Byrd III (September 6, 1728 – January 2, 1777) He inherited his family's estate of approximately 179,000 acres of land in Virginia and continued their planter prestige as a member of the Virginia House of Burgesses. He chose to fight in the French and Indian War. In 1756 he was colonel of the Second Virginia Regiment. William Byrd III had a reputation as a notorious gambler. He initiated what was said to have been the first major horse race in the New World. After he squandered the Byrd fortune on building a magnificent mansion at Westover Plantation, gambling, and bad investments, Byrd III parceled up much of the land he had inherited from his father and sold it off to raise money to pay his debts. He also sold the enslaved African laborers who had worked on his estate. Although his sale of land and slaves generated a huge sum it still was not enough to pay off his creditors. Later, Byrd resorted to a lottery, the prizes of which would come from his estate, Belvidere, at the falls of the James River. However the lottery failed to generate sufficient revenue. Despondent and nearly broke, Byrd III committed suicide on January 1 or 2, 1777.

George Wythe - George Wythe (pronounced WITH) (1726 – June 8, 1806) was the first American law professor, a noted classics scholar and Virginia judge, as well as a prominent opponent of slavery. The first of the seven Virginia signatories of the United States Declaration of Independence, Wythe served as one of Virginia's representatives to the Continental Congress and the Constitutional Convention. Wythe taught and was a mentor to Thomas Jefferson, John Marshall, Henry Clay and other men who became American leaders.

Chapter 3

Edmund Pendleton - Edmund Pendleton (September 9, 1721 – October 23, 1803) was a Virginia planter, politician, lawyer and judge. He served in the Virginia legislature before and during the American Revolutionary War, rising to the position of Speaker. Pendleton attended the First Continental Congress as one of Virginia's delegates alongside George Washington and Patrick Henry, and led the conventions both wherein Virginia declared independence(1776) and adopted the U.S. Constitution (1788)

Chapter 4

Jacky Custis - John Parke Custis (27 November 1754 – 5 November 1781 The son of Daniel Parke Custis, a wealthy planter, and Martha Dandridge Custis, he was most likely born at White House, his parents' plantation on the Pamunkey River in New Kent County, Virginia. Following his father's death in 1757, almost 18,000 acres of land and about 285 enslaved Africans were held in trust for him. In January 1759, his mother married George Washington. The Washingtons then raised him and his younger sister Martha (Patsy) Parke Custis (1756–1773) at Mount Vernon. Washington became his legal guardian, and administrator of the Custis Estate. Upon his sister's death in 1773 at the age of seventeen, Custis became the sole heir of the Custis estate. Jacky was said to be troubled, lazy and a "free-willed" child who took no interest in his studies.

Chapter 5

Dr. Benjamin Rush - Benjamin Rush (January 4, 1746 – April 19, 1813) was a Founding Father of the United States. Rush was a civic leader in Philadelphia, where he was a physician, politician, social reformer, humanitarian, and educator as well as the founder of Dickinson College. Rush attended the Continental Congress and signed the Declaration of Independence. He served as Surgeon General of the Continental Army and became a professor of chemistry, medical theory, and clinical practice at the University of Pennsylvania.

Philip Schuyler - Philip John Schuyler, November 10, 1733 – November 18, 1804) was a general in the American Revolution and a United States Senator from New York.

Charles Lee - Charles Lee, January 26, 1731 – October 2, 1782) served as a general of the Continental Army during the American War of Independence. He also served earlier in the British Army during the Seven Years War. Lee moved to North America in 1773 and bought an estate in Virginia. When the fighting broke out in the American War of Independence in 1775, he volunteered to serve with rebel forces. Lee's ambitions to become Commander in Chief of the Continental Army were thwarted by the appointment of George Washington to that post.

Chapter 6

General Greene - Nathanael Greene (August 7, 1742 – June 19, 1786, sometimes misspelled Nathaniel) was a major general of the Continental Army in the American Revolutionary War known for his successful command in the Southern Campaign, forcing British Lieutenant General Charles Cornwallis to abandon the Carolinas and head for Virginia. When the war began, Greene was a militia private, the lowest rank possible; he emerged from the war with a reputation as George Washington's most gifted and dependable officer. Many places in the United States

are named after him. He suffered financial difficulties in the post-war years and died in 1786.

Chapter 7

Colonel Knox - Henry Knox **(July 25, 1750 – October 25, 1806) was a military officer of the Continental Army and later the United States Army, who also served as the first United States Secretary of War from 1789 to 1794.**
Born and raised in Boston, Massachusetts, when the American Revolutionary War broke out in 1775, he befriended General George Washington, and quickly rose to become the chief artillery officer of the Continental Army.

Colonel Ethan Allen - Ethan Allen **(January 21, 1738 - February 12, 1789) was a farmer, businessman, land speculator, philosopher, writer, lay theologian, and American Revolutionary War patriot, hero, and politician. He is best known as one of the founders of the U.S. state of Vermont, and for the capture of Fort Ticonderoga early in the American Revolutionary War along with Benedict Arnold.**
In the late 1760s disagreements with both New York and New Hampshire led to the formation of the Green Mountain Boys that later became a fighting unit in the Continental Army.

Phyllis Wheatley - Phyllis Wheatley **(1753 – December 5, 1784) was the first published African-American female poet. Born in West Africa, she was sold into slavery at the age of seven or eight and transported to North America. She was purchased by the Wheatley family of Boston, who taught her to read and write and encouraged her poetry when they saw her talent. In 1773 The publication of her** Poems on Various Subjects, Religious and Moral **brought her fame both in England and the American colonies. Figures such as George Washington praised her work.**

Chapter 8

General Putnam - Israel Putnam **(January 7, 1718 – May 29, 1790) was an American army general officer, popularly known as** Old Put, **who fought with distinction at the Battle of Bunker Hill (1775) during the American Revolutionary War (1775–1783). His reckless courage and fighting spirit became known far beyond Connecticut's borders through the circulation of folk legends in the American colonies and states celebrating his exploits.**

Chapter 9

Robert Morris - Robert Morris **- January 20, 1734 – May 8, 1806), a Founding Father of the United States, was a Liverpool-born American merchant who financed the American Revolution and signed the Declaration of Independence, the Articles of Confederation, and the Constitution. As the central civilian in the government, Morris was, next to General George Washington, "the most powerful man in America." His successful administration led to the sobriquet, "Financier of the Revolution."**

Chapter 10

Massacre at Paoli – **The Battle of Paoli (also known as the Battle of Paoli Tavern or the Paoli Massacre) was a battle in the Philadelphia campaign of the American Revolutionary War fought on September 20, 1777, in the area surrounding present-day Malvern, Pennsylvania.** The cry "Revenge the Wayne Affair" **became a battle cry of Continental forces in several subsequent battles.**

Chapter 11

General Gates - Horatio Lloyd Gates (July 26, 1727 – April 10, 1806) was a retired British soldier who served as an American general during the Revolutionary War. He took credit for the American victory in the Battles of Saratoga (1777) – a matter of contemporary and historical controversy – and was blamed for the defeat at the Battle of Camden North Carolina in 1780. Gates has been described as "one of the Revolution's most controversial military figures" because of his role in the Conway Cabal, which attempted to discredit and replace George Washington.

Chapter 13

Colonel John Laurens - John Laurens (October 28, 1754 – August 27, 1782) was an American soldier and statesman from South Carolina during the American Revolutionary War, best known for his criticism of slavery and efforts to help recruit slaves to fight for their freedom as U.S. soldiers. Laurens gained approval from the Continental Congress in 1779 to recruit a brigade of 3,000 slaves by promising them freedom in return for fighting, but the South Carolina legislature killed the plan. He was killed in the Battle of the Combahee River in August 1782, one of the last battles of the war.

Chapter 14

General Sullivan - John Sullivan (February 17, 1740 – January 23, 1795) was an American General in the Revolutionary War, a delegate in the Continental Congress, Governor of New Hampshire and a United States federal judge. He served as a major general in the Continental Army and as Governor (or "President") of New Hampshire. He commanded the Sullivan Expedition in 1779, a scorched earth campaign against the Iroquois towns that had taken up arms against the American revolutionaries.

Chapter 15

Champe - Sergeant Major John Champe (1752 – 1798) was a Revolutionary War senior enlisted soldier in the Continental Army who became a double agent in a failed attempt to capture the American traitor General Benedict Arnold (1741-1801).

Chapter 18

James Armistead - James Armistead Lafayette (December 10, 1760 – August 9, 1830) was an enslaved African American who served the Continental Army during the American Revolutionary War under the Marquis de Lafayette. As a double agent, he was responsible for reporting the activities of Benedict Arnold – after he had defected to the British – and Lord Cornwallis during the run-up to the Battle of Yorktown. He fed them false information while disclosing very accurate and detailed accounts to the Americans.

Chapter 19

Free African Society - The Free African Society, founded in 1787, was a benevolent organization that held religious services and provided mutual aid for "free Africans and their descendants" in Philadelphia. The Society was founded by Richard Allen and Absalom Jones. It was the first Black religious institution in the city and led to the establishment of the first independent Black churches in the United States.

Lafayette's Experimental Slave Farm - Lafayette asked Washington to consider a joint venture for gradual emancipation, but as it turned out Lafayette would conduct the experiment alone in the French Colony of Cayenne in South America. In 1785 Lafayette acquired a clove and cinnamon plantation in present day French Guiana. Here he accomplished the "gradual emancipation" of nearly seventy slaves aged between 1 and 59. The enslaved laborers were paid for their labor, were provided with education, and punishment for them was no more severe than for white employees. Lafayette hoped to show that productivity and birth rate would rise, and infant mortality would decrease under these "humanitarian" conditions, thus demonstrating the inutility of slave trade for economic exploitation. From then on he became part of an international network of abolition activists.

Chapter 22

Hercules - Hercules – also known as "Herculas" or "Uncle Harkless" – was a slave who worked at Mount Vernon, George Washington's Virginia plantation on the Potomac River. He was the head cook at the mansion in the 1780s, cooking for the Washington family and their guests. In 1790 President Washington brought him to Philadelphia, Pennsylvania (then the temporary national capital) to cook in the kitchen of the President's House. Hercules escaped to freedom from Mount Vernon in 1797, and later was legally manumitted under the terms of Washington's will.

Oney - Oney "Ona" Judge (c.1773—February 25, 1848), known as Oney Judge Staines after marriage, was a mixed-race slave on George Washington's plantation, Mount Vernon, in Virginia. Beginning in 1789, she worked as a personal slave to First Lady, Martha Washington in the presidential households in New York City and Philadelphia. With the aid of Philadelphia's free black community, Judge escaped to freedom in 1796 and lived as a fugitive slave in New Hampshire for the rest of her life. More is known about her than any other of the Mount Vernon slaves because she was twice interviewed by abolitionist newspapers in the mid-1840s.

Epilogue

George Washington Parke Custis - George Washington Parke Custis (April 30, 1781 – October 10, 1857) was a Virginia plantation owner, antiquarian, author and playwright. The grandson of Martha Washington and step-grandson and ward of George Washington, he and his sister Eleanor grew up at Mount Vernon and in the Washington presidential households. Upon reaching age 21, Custis inherited a large fortune from his late father, John Parke Custis, including a plantation in what is now Arlington, Virginia. High atop a hill overlooking the Potomac River and Washington, D.C., he built the Greek revival mansion, Arlington House (now Arlington National Cemetery) as a shrine to George Washington

Who inherited Mount Vernon? - Bushrod Washington (June 5, 1762 – November 26, 1829) Nephew of George Washington inherited Mount Vernon upon Martha's death. He was an attorney and politician, appointed as Associate Justice of the Supreme Court of the United States, where he served for more than 30 years. He was among the founders of the American Colonization Society in 1816, intended to promote emigration of freed slaves and free blacks to a colony in Africa, and served as its president until his death.

Acknowledgements

I am indebted to my friend Frits Geurtsen for reading and editing several drafts of this book. His insights and encouragement were significant to its final form. He was especially helpful in helping me find and settle on William's voice.

Also to Lois Faber who I'm sure had no knowledge of how much she encouraged my writing.

To Dr. Robert M. Johnson, a prolific writer of historical fiction, for his assistance with publication.

To my wife, Susan Wolff, for her comments, usual enthusiasm, and final editing.

Made in the USA
Columbia, SC
29 August 2017